BOOKS BY DAVID R. LOW

CoinciDATE

SCHLOCK: *Featuring Russia Cop*

The American Brain

DAVID R. LOW

THE AMERICAN BRAIN

Kharms & Bowler Publishing

THE AMERICAN BRAIN

Kharms & Bowler Publishing

ISBN: 978-1-7362773-3-1 (print); 978-1-7362773-4-8 (eBook)

First Edition, 2025

Cover design by Alfred Obare

For the American people

The first individual occurred when cells without nuclei shifted to cells with nuclei.

The next major transition was from single-celled organisms to multicellular ones.

Solitary hunters formed groups. The singular group was one individual, distinguished from other individual groups.

The next major evolution of the individual occurred in 2026— far earlier than anyone could have predicted.

1859

James Dwight Dana wiggled his toes in the sand. The sound of the tide was soothing, even if the weather had taken a turn for the worse, and the longer he played along the shore, the harder it would be to make it to shelter in time. The Gilbert Islands were home to the largest coral atoll in the world, a fact that was not unimpressive to Dana. Straddling the equator, one was greeted with the privilege of witnessing the bend of the Earth. He was fond of his strolls, watching as the southern end of the island vanished as he moved northward. What could be said of the unfathomably turquoise waters that gently graced the shore? The sea was a shade of blue more beautiful than any woman's eyes. Still, after the majestic volcanoes of the Hawaiian Islands, he yearned for the departure to Fiji, where he could continue his research.

He stuck his hand in the sand. Once he brought it back up, he let the pulverized rock fall slowly. He elected to let the minuscule sand crabs emerge on their own rather than harm the delicate creatures. Three of them rested comfortably, engulfed by his fingers.

Dana, a geologist by trade, was eager to get back to the Hawaiian Islands to continue his research on volcanoes, but during his sailing of the seas, he found himself irresistibly fascinated by crabs.

Fernando, one of the deckhands' sons, ran over excitedly. The boy, no more than six, stuck out his hand so Dana could give him the crabs.

"Be gentle, lad, understand?"

Fernando laughed. He laughed every time he heard Dana speak English. The boy knew no English, and Dana knew even less Portuguese.

"Gentle, gentle," he said softly. "See?" He showed the child the gentle way he held the crabs.

Fernando accepted them and let them roam his hand.

"Good lad," said Dana. "It's absolutely remarkable."

The boy laughed again.

"Remarkable," he repeated.

"Remarkable!" said Fernando, amusing himself.

"I've documented hundreds of crustaceans throughout the Pacific. Despite different evolutionary paths, these little fellows —eons along the journey—arrive at similar destinations. They always tend toward a crab look. Their characteristic feature being that of an enlarged head. Curious, isn't it? Is this crab shape the ultimate form of evolution that life leads toward? What do you think, Fernando? Does evolution have a determined destination? It isn't just little friends like our crabs here branching about aimlessly. It almost seems divine, doesn't it? I would wager, Fernando, that everywhere you look—beyond these tiny crabs and you and I—all living matter and everything in nature, yearn to become a brain. It doesn't just wander like infinitely expanding fractals with infinite variables. It tends toward a direction. What do you say to that?"

Fernando laughed, threw the crabs in the water, and ran off.

In an 1863 letter addressed to Charles Lyell, Darwin had the following to say about Dana: "To carry on analogous principles (for they are not identical, for in Crustacea the cephalic limbs are brought close to the mouth) from Crustacea to the classification of Mammals seems to me madness."

2026

Akseli had been at Stanford for two days. For him, going to the United States at that point in time was like traveling to a land of myth and legend, but not in a way that was endearing or inspired intrigue. The news cycle was rampant with absurd stories taking place in America: some new despotic law, some new violation of human dignity, a charlatan pushing antiscience rhetoric. It was like watching all the silliest cartoons of his childhood brought to life. Seeing it with his own eyes was a shock to the system.

What struck Akseli as odd was that his first day on campus, he was given instructions that as a PhD candidate, he was required to submit work for review to the America First Conference of Scientific Breakthrough and Discovery. What it sounded like was the piling on of more work on top of his dissertation.

Despite reservations regarding his own health and safety,

the United States was second to none in the field of neuro-science research.

Inside the laboratory, he caught a glance of his thesis advisor, Dr. Singh. He was unable to speak with him. While observing one rat telegraph to another the correct lever to pull via brain-to-brain interface, Akseli couldn't help but think about the American brain.

It was while ordering his first coffee in the US that a barista, noticing his accent, asked where he was from. When he answered Helsinki, she gave a blank stare. It's the type of stare he noticed among Americans who share a lack of curiosity about the world—a type of gormless, slack-jawed expression. He explained Helsinki was not far from the Russian border.

At that, she asked, "Could you say something in German?"

"German?"

"Yeah", she said.

"I apologize, but I don't speak German," he responded.

"But didn't you say you're from Russia?"

He took the coffee and retreated from the conversation.

Such encounters compelled him to take to drink. At one of the quiet off-campus pubs, there was a billiard table on the bottom floor not being used. Most students had a drink while working on their laptops or poring over notes. Beyond students, old regulars sat nursing drinks and taking in whatever the television behind the counter had to offer.

The news was playing the same footage on repeat of the Supreme Court overturning the Refugee Act of 1980. The president had made various press conferences over the past week, detailing how those given refugee status, starting in 1980, and all their descendants, US citizens or not, would be summarily rounded up and deported. From the looks of it, the studying scholars were unbothered by the changing policies. The old-timers made their approval known to the world and toasted to a bright future.

During a tour of the campus, Akseli noticed DHS agents posted at various corners throughout the campus. One foreign student told him he'd been subjected to a random security search eight times in the same day.

Akseli struggled to reconcile such draconian policies with a country that boasted universities of Stanford's caliber. While inside the lecture halls and laboratories, the noise of the outside world disappeared.

During a brief break, another international student had shown Akseli various YouTube videos where someone on the far left would debate twenty on the far right, or vice versa. Americans, he noted, could be quite contradictory individuals. If he were to base his entire opinion on the populace with only these videos as evidence to go by, his conclusions would be dire. Far-right movements had taken hold in Europe as well; he couldn't claim this was a uniquely American phenomenon. What was uniquely American was the cognitive dissonance he observed. In one breath, he watched as debater after debater would claim universal support for the constitution so long as it benefited his candidate and then would condemn it the moment he was presented with evidence that his preferred candidate was violating the constitution.

Thoughts like this kept him from making any real progress on his thesis. Akseli recognized a face from the brain-to-brain-interface demonstration, a young man in spectacles who looked to be East Asian. The young man made his way over to Akseli.

"Mind if I join you?" he asked.

"Please," Akseli indicated the empty seat.

The television behind the bar coverage continued its coverage of the Refugee Act.

"I'm Jun," he said.

"Akseli."

They shook hands.

Jun had come to Stanford from Busan little over a year ago. He was studying computation with neural bioelectric networks. When Jun asked Akseli where he was from, the Finn shared his encounter with the barista.

"Normally, I'd have laughed, but be careful what you say about America these days."

"What do you mean?" asked Akseli.

Jun scanned the environment.

Is he looking for eavesdroppers? Akseli suddenly felt nervous, regretting receiving the fellow student so readily. *Can't I go five minutes in this country without ending up in some anti-American conspiracy?*

"I mean, I was given an official warning letter from the admissions office about a comment I made."

"What comment?" asked Akseli.

Once more, Jun looked around.

"A picture on my Instagram from the time I was in Baton Rouge and swam in the Gulf of Mexico."

"I'm waiting for the punchline," said Akseli.

"There's no punchline."

"Then perhaps this is some humor I'm not smart enough to understand. What's the issue?"

"Let me read the warning letter I received," said Jun. "*As a foreign student, it is a privilege, not a right, to study in the United States of America. While you may have received your visa before student visa interviews were cancelled, it does not mean you have free rein to criticize or make a mockery of American culture, civil society, sensibilities, or morality. You deliberately displayed anti-American sentiment when posting 'The Gulf of Mexico' on your Instagram account as opposed to its official, legal name, The Gulf of America. Furthermore, making any mention of land situated between a river and the sea is viewed as anti-Israel sentiment. These transgressions are blatantly anti-American and un-Christian. Another warning will result in your immediate expulsion and deportation.*"

Akseli wanted to call the story nonsense, or perhaps something lost in translation, but what motivation would Jun have to trick him? Jun's English was just as good as Akseli's. He didn't look up, but he got the growing feeling that every eye in the room was on him. *Had I been speaking too loudly?*

"Beyond that," continued Jun, "anyone who even dreams about uttering the word Palestine or saying anything slightly out of step with the current mainstream thought is cooked."

"What do the American students think of all this?" asked Akseli.

"I avoid them. Have you noticed that expressionless stare among them? I've heard reference to the Gen Z Stare, but I think this is something else. When a cat looks at you, I'm certain its comprehension is greater. Frankly, Americans scare me. There's something about them, some kind of propensity for cruelty, a constant desire to want others to suffer. I can't wait to get my degree and get out of here."

2026

It didn't matter what the weather was, who the company was, or the casualness of an event; Robert Van Dorn always tucked his shirt in. He also lectured his son—and anyone else's—for not doing likewise and failing to iron their shirts. Cleanliness was next to godliness. He considered himself a patient man, but untidy clothing and the way his children presented themselves to the world were laurels he held strict adherence to.

The Van Dorns lived in a three-story colonial-style home and could trace their ancestry all the way back to the colony of New Amsterdam. As far as Robert Van Dorn was concerned, being Protestant and being loyal to the United States went hand in hand. Luckily for Robert, his neighbors, the Cloverlys, were Protestant. Even if he found their personalities on the annoying side, he knew where he stood with them. His wife, on the other hand, mingled with Catholics and Jews and the sort. She had a bad habit of striking up conversations with everyone and anyone at the check-out line. Being American, as Robert understood, was something earned. Muslims, Jews, and Hindus might have a little piece of parchment that has "America" written on it, but they were nothing more than visitors in this great, sacred land.

Their being nice had nothing to do with whether Robert found them contemptible. It was a question of understanding. He couldn't reconcile how they could reconcile being American and Godless heathens in the same breath.

Missus Van Dorn was entertaining the guests, giving a diet pop to Ainsley Cloverly and a domestic beer to Albert, the husband. Robert Van Dorn was a teetotaler, but he didn't believe it to be his place to tell another man what he could or couldn't put in his body.

Albert had a round, red face even without alcohol consumption. Missus Van Dorn had given up on trying to make her husband and Albert friends outside of neighborhood gatherings. If they wanted to come over to discuss sports or the economy, Robert would do it from the comfort of his own chair.

Robert sat down right as the front door opened, and his teenage daughter, Lauren, walked in and started upstairs without greeting a single guest.

"She's a sulky one, isn't she?" asked Ainsley.

"Say hello to the guests," said Missus Van Dorn.

"Hello," she said, halfway up the stairs.

"I didn't raise you to be rude. What's with the sulking? How was work?" asked Robert.

"I'm quitting," she said.

"After your first day? Is that the work ethic Benjamin Franklin instilled in the nation?"

"Now that was a fine president, a fine president," said Ainsley Cloverly.

"Dad, you don't get it. I don't want to hear about how waiters in your day had enough to buy a house and two cars. Did you know they lowered the minimum wage for tipped employees to only a dollar? That's slavery!"

"I wouldn't have been caught dead working as a waiter. I'd have gotten a real job. And it isn't slavery," said her father.

Missus Van Dorn was setting clean plates in the cabinet above the stove, but it might as well be an elephant rummaging through the house, what with the level of grace she had. If Robert were to shut the door a little too loudly on the way to work, the Missus would let him know about it till Easter, but God forbid he tried to watch TV or have a conversation without her slamming cabinets and smacking ceramics.

"You know," said Albert. "All things considered, slavery wasn't that bad. If it weren't for slavery, those poor souls would still be stuck in Africa. Let me ask you, who's living the better life, Blacks here or Blacks there? If anything, they should be grateful they were brought over here."

"I didn't raise my child to be a whiner." Robert stopped to look at his wife. The woman had the magic ability to pull dishes out of thin air. *How long does it take to put dishes away?*

"You get tips, don't you? If you don't like the wages, work hard and with a smile. Make those customers want to hand over their hard-earned money to you. You kids have no idea how easy you've got it. You think it's hard, do you? This is a free market; if you don't like it, find work somewhere else."

"Where?" she pleaded, tears in her eyes. "Where, exactly? Nontipped jobs are no better since Michigan lowered the minimum wage to five dollars. Five dollars, Dad!"

"I never thought I'd hear my daughter asking for handouts. Go to your room and think of something smart to say before you come back out."

"The mouth on her," said Ainsley.

"We were young once," said Mrs. Van Dorn.

"But not like that. Work ethic indeed, my word," said Ainsley.

"You hear about the Donolons' exchange student?" asked Albert.

"That little Russian kid?" asked Robert.

"Russian? Or Siberian. Serbian. One of those Russian countries. Anyway, he was sent packing."

"What do you mean?" asked Robert.

"State Department said his visa was no good. Pack your bags, kid! You're going home."

"Oh, he was such a polite boy," said Missus Van Dorn.

"I, for one, am glad he's gone," said Albert. "Why should we be funding kids who aren't even from here to study in place of our own? If their countries are so great, they should stay and study there."

"Polite or no," said Robert. "These students. They abuse our hospitality, you know? It's well and good that they want to study in the US, because who in their right mind wouldn't? But they abuse the hospitality of our people. They speak their own languages in public, saying God knows what. They receive benefits without paying taxes, and then they take part in anti-American rallies and propaganda meetings that these leftist schools endorse. If they aren't ready to fully embrace our American culture, then good riddance. Send them packing. We don't need 'em."

"I hear what you're saying, but he was such a nice boy. Remember, he helped Junior with his chemistry homework," said Missus Van Dorn.

"Stop telling me what I remember. I don't remember that," said Robert.

2027

Akseli Holopainen got the distinct impression his thesis advisor hated him. Others had warned Akseli not to take it personally, as Dr. Singh didn't like anybody. Akseli couldn't bear watching Dr. Singh go over his work. He looked around Dr. Singh's office, but it was so minimally decorated that Akseli understood nothing was coming to save him. Dr. Singh didn't even have his own publications lining the spartan shelves. Singh had published with Joseph E. LeDoux and had more sympathy for the rats whose brains he operated on than the living humans who were under his tutelage. He was famous for his ruthless rejections, always leaving it up to the rejected to discover the means of their failure rather than offering an explanation.

Despite being over a full foot taller than the man, Akseli was deathly afraid of Dr. Singh. Dr. Singh had the magic ability to digest an entire page of information with only a two-second glance.

"Drivel," he said. "Come back later."

"If I may ask—"

"You may not."

"Sir, I'm exhausted."

"If you were as keen on authoring compelling research as you were at testing my patience, you might have something worth discussing. What's there to say? You go on about temporal binding and feature binding as though they're unrelated phenomena. Do you suppose this is still 1993? Are you so thick as to think nobody has bothered to integrate them into a unified theory? You've made no meaningful contribution in your work, and don't mistake ambition for comprehension or contribution. Now leave me alone, for God's sake."

Masked men burst through the door.

"Wait a min—" Singh was unable to finish his sentence.

The masked assailants smacked him across the face and pinned him to his desk. Akseli sat in silence, feeling like a coward for doing nothing and feeling grateful for being ignored.

The men roughed up Dr. Singh while looking for whatever it was they were in search of. Other men tossed what little was in the room on the ground. Akseli heard several pages being torn.

"Passport," one of the men demanded.

Dr. Singh handed his passport to the man. The man opened the small blue book.

"This is the fifth time this week I've been forced to show my passport. I'm an American citizen."

"For now," said the masked man, tossing the passport on Dr. Singh's desk.

The men left without explanation. Dr. Singh didn't blink for two minutes.

Akseli had entered the room fearing the doctor, but left feeling deep sorrow for him. Akseli later learned that fifty students had been rounded up that day and disappeared.

Even with the masked men interrupting, the meeting went about as well as Akseli expected. The truth was, he had long ago abandoned his original thesis plan of attempting to solve the unity of consciousness and binding problem with something even more radical and fantastical. It was so out there, in fact, that if he ever let any of his peers or mentors know what he was researching, he'd be laughed all the way back to Finland. He woke up most mornings believing himself crazy. The implications, however, of his theory proving to be true were apocalyptic.

Either commit fully or quit, he repeated. *But how arrogant!* he rebutted. *How arrogant that you, and you alone, are on the verge of this massive scientific breakthrough.*

Consciousness. Is it a question of consciousness? The hard problem of consciousness never kept him up at night the way it did now. Theories proposing that consciousness doesn't originate from the brain were so impossible to test, let alone prove. *So why bother?* But he couldn't help but entertain the idea that a force was at play affecting the American brain. But what if it came from within, rather than without?

After playing a game of pickleball with (and getting decimated by) Jun, Akseli took a quick shower and went to the library. After his first meeting with Jun, Akseli amused himself by looking for the slack-jawed Americans on campus. He saw them when they didn't like a professor's explanation, and he noticed them when they were all by themselves, either staring at their phones or looking off into space. What started off as innocent amusement began to take a more sinister turn. *Is something wrong with them?*

While searching for the materials Singh gave him, Akseli caught himself staring at a slack-jawed American and retreated into the shelves after being spotted. Once the coast was clear, he set out to leave, but a thick volume by James Dwight Dana caught his eye. Reading for pleasure was the last thing he had any time for, but he found himself drawn to Dana's ideas, especially those concerning nature's will for evolution driving toward some specific goal.

His research was taking him into the realm of pseudoscience, into a realm no self-respecting neuroscientist dared to go. But the patterns... The patterns were there.

Pseudoscience aficionados for decades thought there to be magic, mystical mushrooms deep in the rainforest that unlocked new brain potentials, such as talking to God, telepathy, communicating with the dead, and so on. Even if it was complete drivel, what was that saying about broken clocks being right twice a day?

Fortunately for the scholar, Stanford was at the forefront of GPCR-based sensor technology. He had grant money to spend, and he was going to get his money's worth. He gathered hundreds of volunteers of all backgrounds and ideologies and monitored their neurotransmitters. Questions in the tests varied from simple cognitive thought experiments, moral conundrums, political opinions, basic maths, and so on.

To further test his hypothesis, he narrowed the next test

group to Americans who identified politically as right of center.

Some of the scenarios presented were quite simple: Should the president, any president, uphold the Constitution? Should the Constitution be respected and followed fully, or only the aspects of it that appeal to you? Is the president above the law? Can the president be prosecuted for convicted crimes while holding office? Is it a crime if the president does it? He moved on to disparate topics, only to eventually return to the previous topics about the president, but this time, rather than talking about the president in the abstract, he talked about the current, right-wing president whom the test subjects proclaimed support for at the beginning of the test.

Akseli, having noted that his presence in the interviews seemed to agitate the participants, decided to bring in student-teacher Anna, whose amicable demeanor made her far more suited to asking the questions than he was. All the questions were prepared for her, but she still wore an earpiece in case he needed her to pose necessary follow-up questions. Akseli monitored the sensors as she engaged with the interlocutors.

The final interviewee of the test was Jacob Milton, 28, from Youngstown, Ohio.

Anna: How do you identify?

Jacob: What?

Anna: Could you please tell me how you identify?

Jacob: Is this some kind of identity politics thing?

Anna: Can you just tell me your age,
religious affiliation (if any), and your
political affiliation?

Jacob: Don't you already know this? I
filled out that form. What was the
point of that form if you're gonna ask
me again?

Anna: Are you Christian?

Jacob: Yes.

Anna: Are you liberal or conservative?

Jacob: I'm conservative.

Anna: Okay. I'm going to ask you a
series of questions that weren't in the
previous form. Answer honestly,
please. There are no right or wrong
answers.

Jacob: And I'll get paid at the end?

Anna: Yes.

Jacob: Alright.

Anna: Do you support the notion
"America First"?

Jacob: One hundred percent.

Anna: And what does "America First"
mean to you?

Jacob: It means we need to stop worrying about what other countries are getting into and worry about ourselves. Stop giving work to illegals, for one. Stop letting some barely-can-speak-English Hindu take all the tech jobs, and stop giving handouts. No more foreign aid to Ukraine, a country so corrupt it doesn't even know where the hundreds of billions of dollars we send it go. That's money we could be giving to American farmers and factory workers. If Ukraine can't win its wars on its own, it never should've gotten into them in the first place.

Anna: So, no foreign aid and a focus on America's own workers?

Jacob: That's right.

Anna: My next question is about law enforcement. Do you think they should be more or less militarized?

Jacob: Definitely more militarized. You've got leftist cities trying to defund the police and tie their hands every chance they get. The police are here to make our streets safe, but with BLM and rioters and the drug addicts, it's getting harder and harder. They need state-of-the-art weapons.

Anna: You see the left as detrimental to law and order?

Jacob: Absolutely, I do. If it were up to them, we'd be living in lawless chaos where anyone could do whatever they want without any consequences.

Anna: Do you believe the Constitution
to be an intrinsic part of U.S. civil
society and that its tenets should be
upheld?

Jacob: I'm a patriot. Of course I do.

Anna: Do you believe the president
should uphold these tenets and be an
exemplary standard of them?

Jacob: I sure do.

Anna: Is free speech important
to you?

Jacob: What a stupid question.

Anna: Could you answer it, please?

Jacob: Of course it's important to me.
It's one of the main things that makes
this the greatest country in the world.

Anna: What are the others?

Jacob: The Second Amendment, the
church, supporting the troops, and the
boys in blue.

Anna: Tell me why free speech is
important to you.

Jacob: It means don't tell me what I can or can't say. If you're offended, that's your problem, not mine. We need to stop catering to these weak sensibilities. A white man can't say anything without a bunch of people flipping out and trying to ruin his entire livelihood. I say black people commit more crimes, you say it's racist. I say okay, let's debate it—but don't try to ruin my life. Let's disagree like adults and talk about the merits of our arguments. You still have to respect my opinion. cancel culture doesn't want to do that. It wants to punish you for something you said, ruin your life, and make it so you can never work again.

Anna: Do you see cancel culture to be a big issue?

Jacob: Definitely, I do.

Anna: Does one side utilize cancel culture methods more than the other?

Jacob: It's leftists! Do you even have to ask?

Anna: I'm going to read a quote for you: "I think it's worth it, I think it's worth it to have a cost of, unfortunately, some gun deaths every single year so that we can have the Second Amendment." Do you know who said that quote, and do you agree with it?

Jacob: Charlie Kirk, and yes, I wholeheartedly agree with it. No system is perfect. Car crashes are gonna happen. Guns are an inherent part of this beautiful culture. If you count up how many guns there are in the country compared to how many people die from shootings, it's relatively small. Guns are a right. When big government steps in, how else are we to defend ourselves?

Anna: Do you believe Christian values are an intrinsic part of American identity?

Jacob: Well, that's a given.

Anna: And do you believe American leaders should reflect Christian morals?

Jacob: Yes.

Anna: Could you tell me what some of those are?

Jacob: Well, praising the Lord. Beyond that, you know, just things that make you a decent person—things the Bible teaches us: honesty, integrity, humility. All that.

Anna: Do you trust the news media?

Jacob: What do you mean?

Anna: What do I mean?

Jacob: Yeah, do you mean the mainstream media? Then hell no, I don't.

Anna: What, in your view, is the
mainstream media?

> Jacob: Media controlled by the deep
> state, the elites—all controlled by,
> well, you know who. Fake news.

Anna: Where do you get your news
from?

> Jacob: I don't read much news, but
> when I do, FOX News is pretty good,
> and Newsmax. I like the stuff I see on
> my feed. It makes sense to me. I look
> at it and I know it's coming from a
> different source than the made-up
> gibberish of the mainstream media.

Anna: What does "Drain the Swamp"
mean to you?

> Jacob: Exactly what it sounds like—
> getting rid of the corruption within the
> deep state. Removing those who've
> run this country into the ground and
> replacing them with those who are
> patriotic, loyal, and demonstrate true
> American values.

Anna: Thank you for your responses.
Now I'd like to circle back. When
discussing "America First" and
suspending foreign aid to countries
like Ukraine, how do you feel about
the fact that this administration gave
$57,000,000,000 in taxpayer money to
bail out Argentina? Doesn't this
contradict the notion of "America
First"?

Jacob: Not at all. He wouldn't give money to bail out a country if they weren't ideologically aligned with us.

Anna: So, Ukraine isn't ideologically aligned with us?

Jacob: Of course not.

Anna: Can you explain how?

Jacob: Ukraine is a warmongering country run by leftist Nazis who started a war with a much bigger, more powerful country, and they can't see the writing on the wall that the battle is lost.

Anna: You think Ukraine is responsible for this war?

Jacob: Who else? Well, them—plus a mix of the Obama and Biden administrations.

Anna: So it's okay this money didn't prevent Argentina's economic collapse?

Jacob: You're twisting words and facts. Anything can look bad if you spin it to fit your conclusion.

Anna: During the 2018 trade war with China, Chinese soybean purchases dropped by 70 percent. By USDA estimates, American farm income fell by more than $11,000,000,000. Crop prices plummeted so severely that farmers were unable to sell their products at sustainable prices. Was this putting America first?

Jacob: The president was standing up
to China—that's what he was doing. If
they're gonna make us pay high
prices, why can't we do the same?

Anna: Even if the effect is Americans
losing mass quantities of money?

Jacob: What's your point?

Anna: Don't you think these policies,
resulting in the loss of revenue, are in
direct contradiction to the idea of
"America First"?

Jacob: It's because the deep state is
always trying to sabotage everything
he's doing. They'll veto his proposals
just to be pricks about it. Like shutting
down the government.

Anna: If I understand correctly, all
three branches are under Republican
control, but the shutdown is the fault
of Democrats?

Jacob: Of course it is.

Anna: Is there any scenario at all in
which you could see any of this being
the Republicans' fault?

Jacob: No.

Anna: You mentioned strong support for law enforcement. The January 6 Capitol Riot included violence against law enforcement, resulting in the deaths of five police officers. How do you reconcile respect for law and order while also supporting a cause that murders police officers?

> Jacob: Your reading of it is all wrong. It was leftist agitators who killed the police officers. They were the violent ones—planted there to make us look bad.

Anna: Were all the rioters that day leftists?

> Jacob: Well, yeah, the bad ones at least.

Anna: But you contend that it was a rigged election, right? Joe Biden did not win that election.

> Jacob: Of course he didn't. It's obvious to anyone. It was a violation of our rights. We knew it, and the true president knew it.

Anna: So he was justified in encouraging his supporters to fight for the truth and take back what's rightfully theirs?

> Jacob: No doubt.

Anna: So storming the Capitol to oust those who rigged the election was a justifiable action?

Jacob: Exactly. It was patriotic. It was
a patriotic protest.

Anna: Just a second. Was it a patriotic
protest, or a bunch of leftist agitators
trying to paint the right in a bad light?

Jacob: I see what you're trying to do,
and I'm not going to play ball.

Anna: Which one is it? If I understood
correctly, the election was stolen.

Jacob: Yes.

Anna: So the president urged his
supporters to reject it. He told them
Biden was illegitimate. They listened
to his words.

Jacob: Right.

Anna: Right. As patriots, they should
demonstrate their patriotism and
loyalty in the form of a patriotic
protest.

Jacob: Right.

Anna: So, if the patriotic protest was
justified, and it happened, but didn't
happen, because it was hijacked by
non-patriots pretending to be patriots
at the same protest that wasn't
actually the protest—then technically
there was a protest, but it wasn't
yours—is that correct?

Jacob: Next question.

Anna: The president eventually pardoned those who participated at the riot and were arrested. Was he right to do so?

Jacob: Well, yeah. Patriots should be rewarded for their loyalty, not punished.

Anna: But wouldn't that mean he was pardoning leftist, paid-actor agitators, not patriots?

Jacob: Next question.

Anna: You described yourself as unequivocally supporting the Constitution and stated it's the job of the president to uphold its tenets. There was no evidence of widespread fraud during the 2020 election, but the president maintains it was stolen—as do many of his supporters—even judges he himself appointed rejected his claims. So, was the election stolen?

Jacob: Of course it was.

Anna: If the shoe were on the other foot, and a liberal candidate made such claims, would they be valid?

Jacob: Look. Defending the president is defending the Constitution. Maybe some drastic measures have to be taken—things that seem like bending the rules—but this is what it takes to fix the nation. We must remain loyal.

Anna: On September 11, 2025, a high school teacher posted the Charlie Kirk quote I shared with you earlier on their social media page. They were then fired.

Jacob: Good.

Anna: Why good?

Jacob: It's sick. These leftists celebrating his death. These bloodthirsty lunatics. The man had kids. He was a Christian.

Anna: The teacher in question who posted the quote didn't provide any additional commentary; all they did was share the quote. Why should someone be fired simply for sharing what the man himself said?

Jacob: Oh, come on! You know what they were doing. They were trying to twist the man's words in a sick way to make it seem like he deserved it.

Anna: But isn't this an expression of freedom of speech? Isn't that something Mr. Kirk himself was a huge proponent of? Isn't the fact that hundreds of right-wingers pressured and bullied schools and businesses to fire employees for posting opinions— or, in some cases, direct quotes of Mr. Kirk—to get fired the ultimate example of cancel culture?

Jacob: The man had just died!

Anna: What's the outrage then? Is it
what he said, or the fact that what he
said reflects poorly on his character?
I'm a bit confused.

> Jacob: It's not cancel culture. It's
> consequences.

Anna: So you're not a free speech
absolutist.

> Jacob: I am.

Anna: Do you see my confusion here?

> Jacob: What you're talking about isn't
> a matter of free speech. It's attacking
> a man for his beliefs.

Anna: Regarding guns—you
mentioned that, as Mr. Kirk did,
despite the inevitable gun-related
deaths, it's worth it for the sake of
protection and because owning them
is an inherent right.

> Jacob: Yup.

Anna: Especially against a tyrannical
government, right?

> Jacob: Mhmm.

Anna: At the moment, we have ICE
agents—men in masks who don't
identify themselves—kidnapping
people from their homes, schools,
places of employment, churches;
beating them, subjecting them to
inhumane conditions, deporting them
without any due process. Would you
suggest that these potential victims of
ICE raids arm themselves to defend
against a tyrannical government?

   Jacob: No, this isn't the same at all—
   and I know you know that.

Anna: How so?

   Jacob: These people are illegals.

Anna: How do you explain, then,
instances where these "illegals" are in
court, going through the proper
channels as appointed by judges who
handle this sort of thing, only to be
arrested in front of the judge who just
decided they can be here? So, who's
correct here—the judge or the ICE
agents? They can't both be right.

   Jacob: If they can come here illegally,
   they can leave here illegally. Fuck 'em.

And that's how it carried on till the end.

~~~

In particular, Akseli was interested in any patterns he could
trace during blatant moments of cognitive dissonance. Cogni-
~~~

tive dissonance theory posits that the mere act of choosing modulates the preferences of individuals. *But let's play around a little bit.*

Using the newest biosensors, the readings were strange, to say the least. The dopamine readings weren't just bizarre, but inconsistent, and frankly, not dopamine. *If you aren't dopamine, then what are you, you strange little molecule?* Akseli remembered that dopamine's role as a transmitter in the brain came much later than its discovery. Initially, it was believed to be nothing more than a precursor to other substances, but Arvid Carlsson later demonstrated that this chemical, which regulates pleasure, movement, and motivation, was in fact a neurotransmitter. But did he dare allow himself the possibility of thinking he'd discovered something new?

What was it about this silly little molecule? He isolated the molecule. Just for fun, he referred to it as Molecule USA in his own thoughts. It behaved like a neurotransmitter, but with bizarre properties. It didn't just transmit signals—it changed people: their moods, perceptions, and more. Beyond that, it could make neurons release more dopamine and alter how serotonin receptors responded. The rewiring of motivation and mood networks was drastic. It was even altering gene expression!

Neurotransmitters—the chemical messengers that help brain cells communicate with one another—were first discovered in 1921 by German pharmacologist Otto Loewi. Before Loewi's experiments, it was unclear whether synaptic signaling was chemical or bioelectrical in nature. Loewi's landmark experiment demonstrated that nerves communicate through chemicals.

He proved this by using two frog hearts: one with the vagus nerve attached and the other without it. He placed both hearts in a saline solution. When Loewi electrically stimulated the vagus nerve, the beating of the first heart slowed. He then transferred some of the surrounding liquid from the first heart to the second, causing the second heart's beating to slow as well. From this, Loewi deduced that the vagus nerve released a chemical substance—later identified as acetylcholine.

After extensive testing, engineers came in to adjust Akseli's hardware. The machine, being new, hadn't previously been used so rigorously.

Akseli ran the tests five more times.

He then ran the tests five times on non-US citizens.

For over a year, he labored over the various pieces of evidence of neuronal synthesis and storage identification of structural characterization. He took urine tests to measure neurotransmitter metabolite levels, blood tests, using antibodies to detect and quantify, and every other criteria until he could definitively conclude that he had made a discovery. He hated being right.

2028

It took seven rejections until a senator would finally meet with Akseli. While Senator Urwin from Illinois was far from an expert in the field of neuroscience, he was one of the few elected officials aiming to increase funding for biomedical research agencies.

The senator was an attractive man on the good side of forty and had an amicable smile.

Akseli had prepared his talking points for months and felt he could deliver a concise and compelling explanation.

The senatorial aide left Akseli alone with the senator after leading him to the room.

"Senator, thank you for taking the time to—"

"My old desk was bigger than this one. The person who designed this one clearly never sat behind one. It's weird."

"Yes, sir."

"So you're the whiz kid. Good, you can lend your expertise.

I'm working on a motion to introduce capitalized numbers. My constituents are adamant about this. We have capitalized letters, so why not numbers? We use numbers just as much as letters, don't we? More, even. Look at some of these proposed capital numbers. Thoughts?"

The senator passed a piece of paper with different shapes and sizes of the newly proposed numerals.

"I like these," he said, laying his large finger somewhere on the page. "Actually, some of my constituents want to completely reform our numbers. Did you know our numerals are Arabic? The people aren't happy about that. One step at a time, I guess."

Akseli had completely forgotten his script. He hated himself for even entertaining the idea of number reforms for a second. The senator sensed the Finn's hesitation.

"They say you invented some new chemical?"

"Discovered, sir."

"Oh, they told me you invented one. Inventing always seems more impressive than discovering something, I feel. Have you invented anything before?"

"Well, no, sir."

"How does one discover a chemical?"

"I'm a neuroscientist. In testing my hypothesis, I discovered a previously unknown neurotransmitter."

"What does it do?"

"That's what I wanted to talk to you about. This chemical only exists in American brains, and unlike other neurotransmitters, it's changing. It's evolving rapidly. Faster than we can keep up with."

"So, it's an American chemical?"

"Well, yes."

"That's good, right?"

"Well, no, sir. This chemical has properties not dissimilar to a rapidly evolving and adaptive virus."

"Just give it to me straight. What does it do?"

What Akseli wanted to tell the senator was that he, and every other American, should be deathly afraid. "It's changing Americans."

"How?"

"Well, I don't quite know yet, sir, but it is."

"Can we patent it? I mean, if it's American, can we capitalize on it? Can we sell it? Science is great. We love science here. The problem with science is it consumes more cash than it makes. We want science that brings money in, you know? Tell me what it does."

"Sir, I believe we are on the precipice of disaster. This chemical is going to change Americans, both mentally and physically, and the results will be catastrophic."

"I'm not following. Change them how?"

"I can't quite say yet how, but a change is coming."

"When?"

"I don't know. It can be in several decades, maybe several centuries. Evolution is slow, but I've never seen a brain chemical behave this way before."

"So you're saying there's time?"

"Time? No, there's no time. It's already started."

"But you just said we may not even see the supposed change for a couple of centuries. I'm not seeing the issue here. You're being an alarmist. In fact, I think you discovered a chemical that doesn't do anything at all, and because it has no actual worth, you're trying to cause a stir."

"Sir, if we don't do something about this now, if we don't warn the public, your entire country is doomed. The American populace is going to change, a change they won't be able to come back from."

"I'm going to need actual proof. This all seems quite vague. What are you even talking about? Get out of my office. I've got actual work to do."

~~~

Nobody wanted to listen. Nobody cared. Nobody understood complex theories and couldn't be bothered to concern themselves with problems that were "years away." The second senator Akseli could get to grant him audience told him to get out of his sight and be grateful his visa wasn't being revoked.

It was a Thursday, which meant the new mandatory Allegiance seminar. All students, regardless of discipline or year, were required to attend. The seminar started with the Speaker leading the students in the Pledge. The Pledge was an extended version of the Pledge of Allegiance, known to all American pupils, but included rising to the occasion to combat all things subversive.

After repeating the Pledge, students sat in a semicircle and took turns calling out what anti-American activities or sentiments they'd witnessed throughout the week. After, they explained the steps they took to combat these actions.

After listening to a girl recall her epic act of patriotism in which she staged a massive protest outside of Elementary
~~~

Spanish II, Akseli no longer cared if the American public heeded his warnings. But like all things American, would their impending doom reach out to drag the entire world into the abyss with it?

Akseli had asked Jun to meet with him in the city to talk about his findings. Their meetings had become less frequent. In general, no one at the university had much desire to leave their homes. Arrests and deportations of students were so frequent and arbitrary that people only stepped out when it was completely unavoidable.

None of that seemed to have any effect on the consumers entering and exiting the Hillsdale Shopping Center. Mothers held their children's hands—unconcerned little humans either busy licking their melting ice cream or running to the nearest store, dragging their mothers along. Several delivery trucks pulled up, and men hauled heavy boxes to their department store destinations.

Akseli spotted Jun at the other end of the parking lot. There was nothing quite like American mall parking lots—vast expanses of land where so many homes could be placed, dedicated instead to consumer parking. He went through the tightly packed cars when an ungodly cacophony of discordant sounds tore through the sky.

Two Black Hawk helicopters hovered over the parking lot, seemingly appearing out of nowhere. Masked men in bullet-proof vests rappelled from the airborne vehicles on wobbly ropes. As that was happening, unmarked vehicles screeched into the lot and more masked men spilled out. All of them had guns drawn, making beelines to the nearest brown people they could find.

The masked men did not discriminate between male delivery drivers and mothers with prepubescent children. They shoved guns in their faces, pressed knees on necks, and separated crying children from crying mothers.

Akseli didn't move a muscle. He was invisible to them. Other bystanders watched as people were thrown to the ground and had guns pointed in their faces. Jun, who was also not moving a muscle, received a pistol to the face.

"Why are you doing this?" he asked.

The answer was another pistol whip upside his head.

"Get on the ground," the agent barked.

"I don't understand," said Jun.

The agent shoved the pistol in his face.

"I need backup!" he yelled.

Four more agents came. They shoved Jun to the ground and pressed their knees into his back and neck.

"I'm a student!" Jun shouted. "I have a student visa. I'm allowed to be here!"

"I don't care," said the first agent.

Akseli, still frozen, watched as Jun and forty others were thrown into the backs of unmarked vehicles. Mothers were separated from their children. Once the vehicles were out of sight, shoppers resumed their shopping.

Akseli couldn't move. *You let them take him. You watched and did absolutely nothing.*

But what good could I have done? What single act of defiance would have made any difference?

It doesn't matter. You showed your true colors. Coward.

Weeks passed, and Jun never came back. Akseli could only assume he was either in some detention center or deported to a country he'd never been to. He couldn't shake the feeling that his inaction was directly tied to Jun's fate.

But what good would my going down with him be? He'd appreciate the gesture, surely—but we'd both be fucked. There's nothing anyone could have done. They have guns, and I don't.

~~~

He managed to turn in a thesis work that Dr. Singh begrudgingly accepted. His discovery of a new neurotransmitter was completely swept under the rug. His final work in the US as a scientist was to take part in the America First Conference of Scientific Breakthrough and Discovery, where all the pressing scientific discussions and breakthroughs by top experts were presented and debated, specifically, science that would make the United States safer, stronger, and more prosperous, with the key event being the unveiling of the new, official capital numbers. Akseli, as the token foreign PhD, was there to show the United States embraced international scholars so long as their work coincided with the three aforementioned points.

After his thirty-second allotted time to speak on the potential of new biosensor technologies, he was to use the remaining time to detail how capital numbers would revolutionize the field of biosensor research.

He stood before an audience of three thousand attendees, and who knows how many others were watching the televised broadcast.

He took to the podium and started: "Americans are strange."
~~~

There was some scattered laughter.

"America is the greatest country on Earth. Who agrees?"

The applause was immediate and deafening.

"But even God's Americans have their imperfections, right?"

Once more, there was scattered laughter. Moreover, the faces Akseli could see were confused. That look of noncomprehension was enough he needed to overcome any nerves or inhibitions.

"This isn't a joke or an attempt at cheekiness. Americans, the world over, have a reputation for their exceptionalism, and I mean that in the worst way possible. An exceptionalism highlighted by exorbitant levels of cruelty, stupidity, violence, and indifference to anything and everything that matters.

"To me, nothing illustrates American insanity more than your gun obsession. In 2024, the US experienced 488 mass shootings. I know the definition of what counts as a mass shooting and how many victims there must be for it to qualify may be debatable, but let's simplify things and talk just about school shootings.

"2015 saw 22 school shootings in the US, 20 the next year, 18 in 2017 (that was a good year, it doesn't drop that low again), 43 in 2018, 61 in 2019, 21 in 2020, 36 in 2021, 53 in 2022, 60 in 2023, and so on. Since the year 2000, there have been 670 mass school shootings and 562 deaths. At school. Children, teenagers, adults, teachers. Americans are the only people on Earth who look at this and think guns aren't the problem.

"It's video games, music, violent movies, a lack of religion, too many immigrants, sexual frustration, but not guns. How do we explain this? Americans are so quick to jump to it being a "right" because it's in the Second Amendment of the Constitution, when these same people don't give a damn about rights such as due process or using the US military against its own population and using said military as a police force.

"These same people, and I've conducted interviews with hundreds of them, will look you in the eye and tell you how the Constitution matters when it involves guns, but doesn't when it comes to the president's suppression of free speech, because the people talking disagree with their views. 'It's okay to suppress it if I don't like it!' If the president pardons violent criminals, it's fine because he's their guy. If a president of the opposing party does the same, it's criminal and unacceptable. It's convenient to be so selective about which rights are considered sacred and which aren't. Let's not forget that in 1776, it took a skilled individual up to a full minute just to load one bullet into his rifle. The founding fathers never could have predicted the weapons of today, and likely would have had a thing or two to say if they could see they'd mostly be used for shooting people at school, concerts, and movie theaters.

"Your president recently announced his plan to make himself supreme leader for life. A man who you've elected twice and who was made his party's nominee thrice is a man twice impeached and currently has 91 criminal charges. How can this be? This man, who cozies up to dictators and authoritarians, says he wants to replicate their practice in the US, then does it, spitting in the face of the law and the Constitution. Help me understand. Yes, I speak English, but I am, after all, a foreigner in these parts. A man who claims to be Christian on one hand while cheating on every wife he's ever had on the other, including admitting in a recording to sexual assault and paying a porn star to keep quiet about their romantic encounters.

"A man so narcissistic and vindictive that his name belongs under the definition of a sore winner. Even after winning, he can't stop badmouthing the former presidents or the nominees he's defeated. Taking credit for reduced prices that were the result of the previous president's policies while blaming inflation and soaring egg prices that were a direct result of his tariff war, that easily could have been avoided at the feet of the previous president. These are things all easily researchable. All the resources in the world are at your fingertips.

"A free speech absolutist who only invites journalists who ask questions he likes or that make him look good. If a journalist quotes him directly, but it paints him in a way he deems not sufficiently worshipful, he attacks the journalist, not the person who said the quote in the first place, himself."

No one in the audience had a face of their own. A single, angry entity stared back at Akseli. The look of pure hatred was palpable. It was a look that dared Akseli to say one more word. Akseli complied.

"When he puts said tariffs on China and allied countries, you know it's you, the citizen, who will pay more for eggs and basic things, right? You know this?

"This man declares himself a 'stable genius,' and because you decided anything he says must be true because he said it, you believe it.

"In a 2019 Fox News poll, a quarter of Americans believed God himself wanted this man to be president.

"Remember when he said he'd end the Ukrainian War in

24 hours and lambasted the previous administration for allowing it to go on as long as it did? Look what happened to the poor Ukrainians.

"What about the claims he built his business from the ground up with nothing more than a measly $1 million loan from his father, when in reality, he got over $413 million from Daddy?

"For no reason at all, claiming his grandfather came from Sweden, when in reality, he came from Germany. What was the point of that one?

"Inventing a public relations persona so he could call tabloids and reporters to report on how much women loved him and how he was so well-liked among celebrities and society at large.

"Claims he passed a veterans benefit law that was signed by his predecessor.

"Windmills cause cancer; that's a personal favorite of mine.

"Thirty thousand five hundred and seventy-three false or misleading statements in his first term as president. You're the same people who got hung up on his opponent's emails for the entire campaign, only to have nothing to say when he brought classified documents to his private residence, but shared them, *shared state secrets*, possibly with foreign adversaries. Instead, you sit there and regurgitate the phrases 'witch hunt' and 'Desperate opposition.'

"He is nothing special. He is not the cause of this country's problems, but a symptom of them. He is the logical endpoint of reactionary, conservative, nationalist philosophy. I'm much more interested in you, the people who made him possible.

"Are you stupid, or are you evil? Option three: Are you all psychopaths?

"The average American pays approximately $477 per month for health insurance. Let that sink in. An estimated forty-five thousand Americans of working age die every year due to a lack of health coverage.

"Let me outline how the US health care system works. A thirty-year-old goes to the doctor because he's sick. The doctor, trained and experienced, prescribes specific medication and a treatment plan. The health insurance providers look at what the doctor prescribed and say, 'This treatment is experimental, we will not cover it,' and so the young man who is paying nearly $500 per month for this health insurance to insure his health, only to be denied, is forced to instead pay $500 for help the provider won't provide, plus $20,000 dollars because the insurance company, arbitrarily, decided they know better than the doctor, dubbing the treatment experimental. And only one percent of denied claims gets appealed. What are we paying $500 a month for if the insurance companies won't help us when we need it? It's the profit. That's all it is and ever was.

"Americans are absolutely terrified of the terms *communism* and *socialism*. The idea of people getting 'hand-outs' sickens them. Free medicine? Absurd. Free education? How dare you! Just look at all those poor, oppressed Scandinavians. What dystopian hell holes they've created for themselves! They all know multiple languages, have higher life expectancies, rate high on the happiness index, have a high standard of living, but clearly, they are jealous of American freedom.

"Americans claim to be free-speech absolutists, but only insofar as it's speech they like. If it's anything that criticizes their beloved president, Christianity, or the flag, then it must be stamped out. They want freedom of religion (so long as it's Christianity, keep your filthy heathen religions away).

"You have a vice president who refuses to condemn the blatantly racist language of the Young Republicans in their group chat. Why should the vice president of the United States need to condemn members of his own party for talking about putting their opponents in gas chambers, praising Hitler, and referring to African Americans as 'watermelon people'?

"I'll tell you why he doesn't condemn it—he doesn't have to. It's no longer necessary to hide bigotry behind sly innuendo. It's out in the open. It's mainstream. It's the status quo.

"And this shows the youth that such thoughts and language are okay. It isn't just okay—it's endorsed. Your leaders *want* you to have these thoughts.

"You have ICE Gestapo thugs kidnapping children—pulling babies from their mothers' arms, attacking citizens and noncitizens alike. Terrorizing U.S. cities, unchecked and unbalanced. This is the big-government tyranny you always spoke of, and you stand by and let it happen.

"Where's the due process? Why do they wear masks? If they're so brave and so patriotic in service to their country, why hide their faces?

"To quote Miguel Ramón Vargas from Orson Welles's seminal work *Touch of Evil*—a film none of you have likely seen, because it came out more than two years ago and you can't be bothered to watch the art that made your country great—'I don't think a policeman should work like a dog catcher.'

"When the corrupt cop, played wonderfully by Welles

himself, argues with Vargas, Vargas counters with, 'In any free country, a policeman is supposed to enforce the law.'

"Orson's corrupt cop isn't convinced. The job is tough, shortcuts have to be taken, extreme measures. Vargas says, 'It has to be tough. A policeman's job is only easy in a police state.'

"Back to your president. 'He loves the veterans!' you say, as he cuts veterans' benefits and lays off hundreds from the Department of Veterans Affairs and veteran suicide hotlines.

"The man who claimed bone spurs to avoid fighting in the Vietnam War, while calling John McCane a loser for being held as a POW. Yet most veterans voted for him. History's most creative and prophetic science fiction writers couldn't come up with a believable explanation for this unprecedented level of cognitive dissonance.

"January 6, the man refused to stand down, is on camera inciting an insurrection, the insurrection happens, and you watch and say it wasn't the man who called for it to happen, but rather the opposition paying people to pose as the opposite party to make them look bad. Where are all these people getting paid, and where can I sign up?

"You scream, 'Epstein! Epstein! He didn't kill himself. Release the files! The Democrats, the Clintons!' Yet when pictures of him with Epstein emerge, and he is mentioned in dozens of documents as one of his best friends, you suddenly don't care about exposing pedophiles at all. How convenient. He was directly involved in using his modeling agency to traffic underage girls. Where's your outrage? What is it you want? What's your ideal conclusion to all this?

"You've all been fooled. And instead of growing and learning, you hold out your hand and say, 'Can I have some more, Daddy? Continue to fool me, please.'

"I ask you here and now, who loves their country less, you or the man you voted for? I'm done. I said what I had to say."

Akseli was punched repeatedly by audience members and police before they arrested him. He spent a month locked up before being deported. The knowledge he had of the ultimate fate of the American people would remain with him.

2029

"How did it go?" Robert asked his wife.

She had been gone since eight in the morning, and it was already nearing 5:00 p.m. Since he left for work early, he liked to eat early, as soon as he got home. His wife's diddle-daddling left him starving. She had tears in her eyes. Those tears didn't stop her from starting the cacophony of unloading the dishes from the dishwasher.

"Now what the heck's the matter with ya?"

"I could kill someone; I swear I could kill someone."

"I'm getting pretty hungry, dear."

"Do you know what they said to me at the doctor's?"

"Well, are you gonna tell me or make me play the guessing game?

"So, I'm waiting and waiting. A complete madhouse. You've never seen the likes of it. People had to wait outside in the cold. After hours and hours, I finally get there, and you know what they tell me? My insurance is no longer accepted. I said the hell it isn't. They said they no longer take Blue Shield. Guy in line next to me says his Kaiser was denied. They explain themselves, 'New policy, we only accept Baron.' I'd never heard of it. So, I says, 'How much is a simple check-up without insurance then?' Know what the bitch behind the counter said?"

Robert lost his concentration, trying to listen through the banging of dishes and slamming of cabinet drawers.

"Know what she said?" she asked again.

"For the love of God, woman, take a seat. I can't hear myself think, let alone your story."

"Know what she said?"

"How could I possibly know? This is your story."

"Five grand! Five thousand dollars! I thought I'd misheard them. Five thousand dollars!"

Missus Van Dorn sat down, only to get back up and start opening more cabinets.

"So, did you do your check-up?"

"What's that, hon?"

"Did you do the check-up?"

"Of course not. I inquired about Baron Insurance. Apparently, it's the only insurance accepted in the entire county. What were we paying, about $350 a month?"

"About $360, yeah."

"About $350, yeah. So, I look online to sign up for Baron Insurance. Can't be done by email; it has to be done by phone. But God forbid they make it easy to find the phone number on the darn site; I'm looking and looking. Finally get it; some robot transfers me five or six times. The representative barely speaks English, I ask to be transferred to someone who speaks English, fairly sure the same guy picked up. I asked for insurance. He says, 'Which tier level?' I says, 'What in the heck are you even talkin' 'bout?' He says, 'There are tier levels.' I just want basic health care, dammit. He says there ain't none. Well. I says, 'I want healthcare that includes basic doctor visits, pre-existing conditions, eyes, and dental.' You know what he did? He starts laughing. I was livid. 'What's got you so tickled?' I asked him. He said 'Ma'am, things have changed. There is no basic health care. Only tiers.' So I says, 'Okay, tell me about the dang tiers then.' He says, 'Tier one covers diabetes.' I say, 'Well, I ain't got diabetes.' He congratulates me and says, 'That's all it covers,' and you know how much it costs? Two thousand dollars a month! Now, I know I don't have diabetes, but I ask if that covers insulin, he says, 'No, it only covers having diabetes,' like, as an idea. Tier two only covers consultations for medica-tion prescriptions. I ask how much it costs. Three thousand a month! Tier three covers basic visits, tier four covers medical emergencies, tier five covers basic visits and medical emergen-cies, but not medication prescriptions. So, I say, 'Okay, what's the one that covers medical emergencies and basic visits as well as medication prescriptions and consultations?' I couldn't believe my ears. There is none! You have to get them all sepa-rately. So someone has to pay up to $8,000 a month for insur-ance? At that point, might as well go to the clinic without any dang insurance.'

She finished putting stuff away and finally sat down.

"Well, now," said Robert. "Nothing worth it is ever easy, now is it?

"I don't know, Bobby, I just don't know. It scares me."

"There's nothing to be scared of. Look at the good the president is doing for our country. Getting rid of all the riffraff and free loaders, people begging for handouts. All beginnings are always a bit rough going. Rome wasn't built in a day, now."

"If you say so, hon."

The next day, Robert Van Dorn was ready to kill his wife.

"I told you not to sign up for any new crap without reading the fine print."

"I didn't sign up for anything."

"You're always scrolling on your phone, opening Lord-knows-what, tagging me in posts, now look."

Robert Van Dorn was looking at a bill of over seven thousand dollars, and for the life of him, neither he nor the missus could figure out where it came from.

"What in God's name is that smell?" asked Robert.

"Why you always got to blame me for stuff?" asked the missus.

"Woman, I'm not blaming you, I'm *asking* you. It smells like pumpkin or some crap."

"Oh, it's probably just part of that new promotion. All houses have it."

"It's making me sick to my stomach. Can't we turn it off?"

"It's pumpkin spice," she said.

"Great, now turn it off."

"Well, I don't think we can. The fridge automatically installed it. Part of the seasonal update. The "Smellness of Wellness" or some such. I don't mind it."

"Oh Lord, is it part of a subscription? I told you to stop clicking stuff. Is that what this 14.99 weekly bill is? Oh, Jesus Christ."

"Well, let me see if I can turn it off then," she said. "It says I have to download the app."

Between the noise of the wife's various notifications and the click-clacking of her fingers and the Starbucks drones bombarding the neighbors across the street, Robert Van Dorn was on the verge of a nervous breakdown.

The fridge could produce the odor of pumpkin spice but refused to open for over a week because the FritoCoins his wife bought, which were sold to her as the most stable new currency, had contracted a virus and were locking all LG smart fridges. Each day, the FritoCoins outgrew the spread of any anti-viral software. The app's customer service told the Van Dorns to download to troubleshoot the issue simply disappeared. Neither of the Van Dorns deleted or uninstalled it; it was simply gone. Trying to google the problem, they were told they did not have enough tokens in their Refund-Master app to perform any Google searches for the next two weeks.

The Starbucks drones played their iconic victory music over their loudspeakers, indicating the housing block had been successfully eliminated. The anthem was instantly recognizable to anyone, but due to one of the drones possibly having taken damage, its melody was a second behind the rest of the drones, creating an ungodly cacophony in the neighborhood.

"Click customer service," she said.

"For what?" Robert couldn't remember which of the problems they had just been discussing.

"The bill," she said.

"Darn it, woman, what do you think I've been doing? Do you see a dang customer service button?"

"I don't have my glasses."

"Don't bother. It's not there. I'll just google this here *Vern*

& Wells Technologies Plus phone number and see what pops up."

He remembered he still had weeks before Google was functional again. He tried his luck by downloading an app with the business's name from the Play Store.

A number did appear, and after he dialed it, he put the phone on speaker. As expected, an automated voice came on. Mr. Van Dorn, out of instinct, immediately started pressing zero, hoping it'd take him to a real person, but the voice kept playing.

"You have reached the officers of *Vern and Wells Technologies*. For information in Spanish, please call 1-866-347-2423, and don't forget to leave your full name, the names of your family members in the household, as well as your current living address. Please listen to the following menu to best select the service you are calling about: If you're calling to sign up for our loyalty program, press one; if you're interested in hearing about offers, sales, promotions, and packages, press two; if you're interested in becoming a sponsor, press three; for international rights and advertising, press four; to hear the options again, press five..."

"I didn't hear anything about refunds—"

"Shhh! Quiet woman."

Robert pressed five to hear the options again, and sure enough, there was nothing about refunds or speaking to a live representative. He pressed one, hoping that it would lead him in the right direction.

"At *Vern & Wells Technologies*, we value all our loyal and dedicated customers. Our loyalty program is a way of giving back. Please listen carefully, as our menu options have changed.

If you are calling about upgrading your tier level, press one; if you have questions about our new seasonal services, press two; if you're calling about a lost or stolen member's badge, press three."

Robert pressed three and was told to hold. When all was said and done, he held for four and a half hours before another soul picked up the other end of the line.

Before the representative could speak, Robert said, "Don't you dare put me on hold or transfer me. I have a bill for seven grand from who knows where, and I want my money back."

"Thank you for calling, sir. Before going forward, we will need you to confirm your identity. We use an NFT-based CAPTCHA system. You will need to hang up and—"

"Now wait a minute, don't you dare end this call. I don't know what that is, you just said," said Robert.

"NFT-based CAPTCHA system is how we confirm the identity of our customers."

"I don't even know what it is I'm a customer of!"

"You got this phone number through the app, correct?"

"Yes."

"Thank you, sir. Now, please log in to your Paramount Plus Authenticator app."

"I don't have one!"

"You will have to purchase one in order to continue."

"How much is that?"

"Before or after the Gatorade tax?"

"What in the Sam Hill are you talking about?"

"Gatorade purchased Wayne County last month, and depending on your district, the Gatorade tax can be as much as fifty percent of the purchase."

The monitor on their washing machine turned on all by itself. The spokesperson was an attractive young woman in a Carl's Junior military uniform, holding a Superstar hamburger in one hand and a rifle in the other. "Don't forget to convert your Medicare points to PrimeMed Tokens by July 15th or risk account suspension! Tokens can be converted from 9:00 a.m. to 10:00 a.m. on Wednesdays and Fridays at select Carl's Junior locations via our in-store terminals after the purchase of any value meal. Customers who purchase value meals via the app are immediately upgraded to Tier two subscribers."

A week passed before Robert was able to get customer service back on the phone after his identity had been verified.

"I see you are a Tier two member. Could you please provide me with your ID number?"

What's going on? Robert put his fingers to the pulse on his neck. *What's happening? Is this what a heart palpitation feels like?* Robert had always believed heart palpitations and the like were made-up malarkey for men of weak moral and mental fiber. His heart was beating louder than the voice on the phone.

"Now listen here, pal, I don't know what this is, but I'm not a member of any club."

"Thank you for clarifying, sir. I see you're calling about a missing badge. All I'll need is some information, and we can get a new one sent out to you."

"You're not listening," said Robert. "What is this? What the heck is *Vern & Wells Technologies*?"

"Thank you for your question. We are a subsidiary of the Department of the Treasury. We—"

"I am not and have never been connected to and have no

relations with the Department of the Treasury. Now listen carefully: I want you to cancel whatever membership you people signed me up for and give me my money back."

"Thank you for understanding, sir. You see, the terms of the contract state that a member must stay a part of their tier group for a minimum of three years before they can terminate the deal. Early termination comes with a fee of five thousand dollars."

"Now hold on, that's nearly as much as the refund. What benefits are there to this program anyway?"

"For every twenty dollars put in, you are rewarded with fifty Amazon Bucks."

"So, where are my Amazon Bucks?"

"Thank you for your question, sir. Pulling up your information, it doesn't look like you've deposited any money into your account yet."

"There's seven thousand dollars in there!"

"No, sir, that money is the deposit for your membership. To maintain your membership and not receive any penalization fees, you must put in a minimum of two hundred dollars per month."

"Wait a minute, you just said—"

"Now, sir, if you'd like to buy Walmart Bucks, you can trade those in for Amazon Bucks with a better return on your investment than with US currency. Furthermore, if you decide to work at one of the Amazon fulfillment centers, you will automatically be promoted to a Tier two member."

"What's the current salary of an Amazon employee?"

"Forty Amazon Bucks per hour, sir."

"I mean in money, dammit!"

"Employees are only paid in Amazon Bucks, but would you like to hear the benefits? I think I heard you say yes. Both Amazon Bucks and Walmart Bucks have their advantages, especially over the US dollar. At Amazon fulfillment centers, the value of an Amazon Buck reflects the amount of work put in. On Mondays, Wednesdays, and every third Saturday, the Amazon Buck has various stimulus benefits. While workers are not paid overtime, every Amazon Buck earned during morning hours on these days goes toward—"

"Please help me," said Robert.

"I understand completely, sir. You've been enrolled in SleepTube Pro. $9.99/month. Auto-renews in thirty seconds. Say 'stop' to cancel."

"Stop," said Robert.

"It sounds like you said *subscribe*. Thank you for your continued business. We—"

Robert hung up. His next phone call was going to be to a lawyer.

2031

The Van Dorns were giving the couple a tour of their new home. No longer able to afford the Colonial in the old neighborhood, they had to settle for a significant downgrade: one story in a neglected neighborhood full of dilapidated old buildings. The missus did her best to make it feel cozy. The Cloverlys, in their stubbornness, refused to vacate when Chick-fil-A bought the surrounding property. Chick-fil-A built its drive-thru that went straight down the center of the Cloverlys' home.

"They deported the Juarez family," said Albert.

"They never did learn English, did they?" asked the missus. "They seemed nice enough, but they never really seemed to become one of us. Always with the loud cucaracha music. How many people lived in their house anyway? All the cousins, aunts, and uncles."

"They were American citizens," said Lauren.

Robert, trying to turn around to face his daughter, got

stuck between the kitchen counter and Albert's stomach. This kitchen wasn't meant for men of Albert's size. Robert would have to make do.

"Then why were they deported?" asked Robert.

"Exactly! It's unconstitutional."

"Well, if they came in illegally, they can leave illegally," said Albert. "The way I see it."

"They were born here!" said Lauren.

"Well, they must have done something un-American. They wouldn't just deport citizens for no reason. Wasn't the father a truck driver? He couldn't speak a lick of English. I know for a fact the president signed some sort of order requiring truck drivers to speak English."

"So now we're deporting people based on whether they can speak English or not?"

"Law's the law," said Albert.

"Deporting American citizens to a foreign gulag is unconstitutional," said Lauren.

"If the president says it's constitutional, it's constitutional."

At that point, Robert Junior ran through the front door, back from one of his jobs. In addition to working for all the different ride-share services, he had employment as an overnight janitor and picked up security shifts at different warehouses when he could get them.

"Did you hear?"

"Hear what?" asked Robert Senior.

"Our old neighbors, the Fennesseys, just packed up their bags and left."

"Where to?" asked Robert Senior.

"Somewhere in Europe, I think."

"And we should care why?" asked Albert.

"It isn't just them. Half the kids I went to school with, they and their families have either already left or are about to."

"No different than COVID," said Robert Senior. "Bunch of sheep panicking over spilt milk and making rash decisions. They're gonna feel mighty foolish when in five years' time, the economy is booming, and the dollar is stronger than it's ever been. Let them have their Europe. Never needed them none, no how. I think the future is bright. It wasn't the end of the world when they banned all them Muslims. Now, we can be true to our roots. Christianity in the classroom again, not being tainted by Islam or atheists. Closing all the embassies and diplomatic missions on the African continent. My brother lives in Minnesota." He turned to Albert. "He said before the closures and bans, walking in his own neighborhood was like trying to cross Somalia or some such. The country is finally beginning to heal."

The following day, Lauren was doing her laundry at her parents' house. Like her brother, she worked more than one job but couldn't afford an apartment with any laundry machines, and all the private machines charged exorbitant prices. Those that didn't charge exorbitant prices had queues exceeding ninety days. Many took to hand washing, but current water bills were nearly as bad as using the privately owned laundromats.

She turned on *60 Minutes* while her father was solving a crossword puzzle and her mother scrolled through her phone.

The elderly gentleman on the television explained to viewers that since January of that year, over ten million Americans have fled the US. The vast majority headed for Canada, with Mexico taking second place. Canada, overwhelmed by the number of recent migrants, was in serious talks of closing its borders entirely to citizens of the United States.

"Turn it off," said Robert Van Dorn. "I don't want fear-mongering nonsense in this house."

"It's the final episode," his daughter said.

The show had been pulled from the air for failing to comply with administrative guidelines.

Albert took that as his cue to leave. Curfew was coming up.

2032

The Van Dorns counted the money a third time.

"It won't be enough," said Missus Van Dorn.

"Just let me talk to them. I'll work something out. Maybe if I give them the money we have, I can make a deal. Work the remaining time left in her stead."

Robert had to sell his truck along with everything in his garage to come up with what amounted to only 40 percent of the required amount.

Albert's son was facing sixteen years of servitude for being unable to pay a speeding ticket and then trying to fight it in court.

Different people were sent to different places, depending on their crime. Lauren's inability to pay back her student loans and credit card debt made her an indentured servant, forced to work off her debts as the CEOs saw fit. For the past eight months, she'd been toiling away in a coal mine in West Virginia.

Coal was coming back in a big way, ever since the America First Energy Act of 2030 banned renewable energies like wind and solar.

Robert Van Dorn waited thirteen hours in line before he was able to speak with an intern. He handed the young man an envelope with the $90,000 in cash and $450,000 in combined Costco Cash and Amazon Bucks. Robert then told the young man his suggestion, to work off the rest of her debt in her stead.

"The thing is, Mr. Van Dorn. You're right that her debt was $170,000 as of last year. But with added inflation, your daughter now owes $430,000. Meaning her sentence is now eight years. You can keep your Costco Cash; it stopped being worth anything since the Best Buy raids. As for the Amazon Bucks, we don't accept them, but if you'd like to convert them to Bumble Tokens sponsored by Mr. Pibb, I can use that to validate your parking."

Due to waiting in line, Robert had missed curfew. While fortunately Doritos enforced their district curfew, Robert still didn't want to push his luck. He'd heard Doritos was becoming just as vicious in their patrols as some of the more notorious enforcement officers, such as Popeyes or Dairy Queen. Loitering came with a fine of $80,000. Always conscientious of following the rule of law, he didn't know what to do. With the money gone, he'd have to have the fun conversation with the missus on how to ration their remaining food.

2033

Lauren had been transferred to another penal colony, and they hadn't heard anything about her since. After writing to the authorities and receiving no word, the Van Dorns accepted they'd never see their daughter again. They still had a son to think about.

Every friend they knew had already fled the country. Only the Cloverlys remained with them.

"Australia and New Zealand are the next countries to close their borders to us," said Albert.

"It's a good thing, then, that we're going to Greece."

Greece, Finland, Dutchland, or Timbuktu, it was all the same to Robert. Home, as he knew it, was long gone. He couldn't remember the last time he'd had a decent night's sleep, so any country that offered that possibility was fine by him. All the same, he tried one last time to convince his wife to tough it out for one more month, just until things got better.

"You know," said Ainsley. "If they treat us as immigrants

even a quarter as poorly as we treated the immigrants who came here, we're doomed."

Nobody was inclined to respond to her sentiment. Both families were leaving a child behind.

The two families grabbed their suitcases. They were sparse, as they had to sell most of their belongings to afford plane tickets.

The airport had no lines to speak of. Crowds of people rushed, pushed, and stampeded over one another. Those who pushed the hardest made it onto their planes, leaving the rest behind.

The planes had people squeezing for space, more reminiscent of the New York subway at rush hour than a commercial flight. None of the restrooms was in operation. With dignity being one of the first casualties, passengers who couldn't hold it went to the toilet, where they stood.

Four hours into the flight over the Atlantic Ocean, the captain made an announcement:

"Ladies and gentlemen. The European Union has drafted a new law, effective as of twenty-two minutes ago, barring all US citizens from entry. In addition to barred entry, American citizens can no longer be present in EU airports for transit purposes. Americans currently in the EU will be duly deported. The plane is being ordered to turn back to its original destination."

2053

The president didn't know how to tell the Secretary of War he hated his mustache. The secretary was well-liked in both the cabinet and the public eye, but the president could not abide by his ridiculous facial hair. The demonstration of military hardware for the guests from Liberia, Burundi, and Mozambique was in less than three hours, and what would they think when they saw the man's offensive facial hair?

He could always make it policy, but Secretary Richter was something of a little bitch. He had a tough exterior, but Baron II knew he was a little crybaby.

Baron II was the youngest president to ever take office, having abolished the minimum age requirement of thirty-five. His dashing good looks and charm made him immensely popular. He was prepared to take on the burden of carrying his family's legacy into the future.

He wished to have stacked his cabinet with equally good-looking chiefs of staff, but they all lacked his youthful flair.

Baron II's servants got him dressed. One of them looked him in the eyes while smoothing out his jacket. He'd have to have the kid executed. Baron II had spent years learning how not to get an erection whenever someone put their hands near his groin region, and that eye contact was too knowing to be forgiven.

Before welcoming the foreign dignitaries, he summoned Hustle Secretary Berman, Secretary of Energy Lange, and Secretary of Christian Affairs Bachman to join him for a ketamine and to discuss the Western problem.

Looking at Lange, Baron II couldn't understand how someone so cool and masculine-looking was so painfully dull, even on ketamine.

"Let's not keep the Blacks waiting. What's new?"

"Mr. President," started Lange. "My brother is requesting more troops to defend the Citadel."

Lange's twin brother was the Viceroy of the Western Corporate Zone. California had become so lawless that the president was forced to use nuclear weapons against it. Just to be sure the threat didn't spread, he firebombed Yosemite and Redwood National Parks. The territory lost its statehood status and was remade as a hybrid military base, Christian holy site, and Amazon fulfillment center.

All three of the western coastal states fell under the dominion of the viceroy, but Lange was doing a shit job at keeping order. Worse, profits were down.

"He's not getting more troops; what he's getting is replaced," said Baron II. He turned to Berman. "What's this I hear about Texas schools using outdated Bertrand capitalized numbers? Can you believe this? Didn't we outlaw those eyesores?"

"It's in all their textbooks," said Berman.

"Those ungrateful, backstabbing sons of bitches. Tell General Matthews to send the 82nd Airborne Division. Burn the textbooks, shoot the teachers. They're this close to losing their statehood status. Bachman, lead us in prayer."

~~~

President Machel of Mozambique looked remarkably cool in his sunglasses, surrounded by his entourage of six-foot-seven armed guards with charcoal-black skin. *See, this is what super soldiers are supposed to look like.* Despite having the best guns and all the money a military force could ask for, time and again, the army let Baron II down. Baron II was certain Machel could maintain the loyalty of his troops even without exorbitant salaries or holding families hostage.

The Colombia Heights neighborhood had been obliterated to make way for grounds for military parades and the demonstrations of weapons. Lining the new grounds were gold statues of Baron II and his family. The bleachers, donated by the president of Somaliland and Papa John's (Musa Aw-Ali Adan was not the president of Papa John's, but he did have a 46 percent share in the company), had been completed in under three weeks. The assembled audience was said to be the largest for a military showcase in human history. In addition to personal friends, there were the most important influencers in the country, business owners, weapons manufacturers and their fami-
~~~

lies, the Boy Scouts of America, and students bused in from schools of all thirty states and corporate zone territories. Four hundred thousand American patriots.

"Dear Leader," said Machel, grasping Baron II's arm in one of those ethnic handshake rituals the leader of the United States would never be able to master.

"Please accept this gift as a gesture of the continued friendship between our two nations."

A soldier handed Machel a long box. The Mozambique president opened it to reveal an absurdly long sword, a blade as tall as Baron II. The handle was golden with engraved rubies and sapphires depicting epic heroes.

"This sword, Mr. President, has personally been used by me to execute traitors, conspirators, spies, drug addicts, dissidents, journalists reporting fake news, and other such nonsense. It has removed the heads of over six hundred and seventy souls. Now I believe when you take a man's life yourself, with a sword rather than a gun, the weapon used traps their soul forever. I would like you to have it. May its strength and yours create something truly epic."

While it was a cool sword, he couldn't help but think that his grandfather had been given a $400 million jet by the Qataris. This sword, at most, would be like a $1 million.

"Come here, Richter, you homo; I'm going to shave your mustache."

"Very good, sir," said Secretary of War Richter.

Holding his new sword, Baron II graced the stage for the adoring audience to behold him. A couple of seconds later, his cabinet joined him on stage, and as agreed, they stood back so they looked smaller to the audience. Baron II refused to use a microphone because he didn't want anything phallic near his face. He also refused the use of headsets because he didn't want any part of his face covered. Therefore, he had state-of-the-art micro-microphones planted all around the stage, so that no matter where he stepped, his voice would be captured and his message conveyed to the audience. Four hundred thousand patriots. *If only it could be five hundred thousand.*

"Americans," Baron II addressed the crowd that had come from all corners of the nation to see him. "This is going to be the greatest parade the world has ever seen. They're already telling me they can see it from space; that's how great the parade is. We have the best toys, don't we?"

He turned to General MacMillan, who smiled in reassurance.

"Just look at how many tanks we have. It's fantastic. I love tanks. Not only do we have the most, but we have the biggest. We like big guns, don't we?"

Baron II was distracted by something happening beyond the fenced perimeter. It looked to be oversize pink pigs, but on closer inspection, he saw they were people. Ten to fifteen enormous, naked lardasses, roaming around on all fours with their faces to the ground, as if grazing.

"What the hell is that?" he asked his chief of security.

"We'll find out, sir."

"I don't want you to find out. Just destroy them. It's totally disgusting."

"Right away, sir."

Sightings of such lardasses had been reported all over the place. The president didn't know what was going on, but it was sick. More than likely, it was some kind of subversive, liberal, deep state plot. They were going to have to try a lot harder to shame him on his day of pride and victory.

After the military march came the reveal of the never-before-seen M1A6 Abrams tanks. They roared to life. Baron II had ordered the engineers to make the engines as loud as possible. To demonstrate their unbelievable accuracy, seven selected tanks from half a mile were all going to fire upon the same target. One of the servants who served flat Coke to Baron II would stand with a Coke can on his head. The seven tanks would aim for the can and fire at the same time. This servant was getting off easy. He had nothing to fear, a testament to both the tanks' precision and the soldiers' dedication.

Baron II looked at Machel, the arrogant bastard. *You may have your soldiers' loyalty, but loyalty isn't enough to win battles. You need the good toys.*

On mark, the tanks fired. They missed spectacularly by over a hundred meters. Baron II could hear Machel's men laughing. Whatever, Greece wasn't built in a day. On the second attempt, they missed by an even wider margin, wiping out a section of bleachers where Boy Scouts had been given exclusive seats.

"Now would be a good time to use the gift I gave you," said Machel, unable to control his laughter.

You won't be laughing once we unveil the new seventh-generation jet fighter, the F-35 Apocalypse.

Baron II waited for their epic arrival. They were to fly low over the audience in perfect formation, scaring the shit out of everyone in attendance. But the sky was silent. He looked over to Machel and saw him grinning. He heard restless audience members shuffling around in the stands.

"Baxter." He turned to one of his aides. "Time to pull out the big guns. We'll give these fools something to laugh at."

"Right away, sir," said Baxter.

Once everyone in attendance saw what the United States had in store, nobody would laugh at him, his presidency, his dynasty, or his country ever again. This project was seven years in the making.

On that cold November day all those years ago, Baron II knew this meeting would change history. He had gathered all his friends, his cabinet, and "the smartest, most loyal scientists in the country," to devise The Goliath.

"What's the largest thing to ever fly?" Baron II asked.

"Living creature or manmade, sir?" some dork responded.

"What's the largest thing to ever fly goddammit?"

Nobody responded.

"I'm fairly sure it was the Hindenburg. Yeah, it was the Hindenburg. Now that was a big thing. I don't see why we don't make everything that big. Bigger. We're going to build the biggest airplane in the world. It has to be at least eight times bigger than the Hindenburg. I want it to scare our enemies and allies alike. It has to represent America. Just looking at it will make people patriotic, and our enemies respect us. You know? I don't know why you aren't writing this down. You should be telling me your ideas. I don't know why I have to be the one telling you this."

"Mr. President, if I may?" some dork scientist stepped in. "The Hindenburg was eight hundred feet long and one hundred thirty-five feet in diameter."

"What's that in capital numbers?"

"I'll draw it out for you. If what you're suggesting is something eight times larger, the material cost would be exorbitant. Then we look at the inherent strength-to-weight ratios with our materials, you know? Aluminum, carbon fiber, and things like this severely restrict how long wings can be. Bigger wings would mean bigger engines. Yes, physics allows scaling up, but the practical and economic factors make such an endeavor nearly impossible."

"Okay, you little weasel, how much would it cost?" Baron II asked.

"Considering the vast sums of materials we would need in addition to constructing a runway large enough, you'd be looking at a cost of upward of $30 billion for something that won't provide any financial return."

"Wrong. It will be the greatest financial investment in history. Have people buy Baron stock. We'll sell NFTs to cover the cost. They'll be great NFTs. People will look at it and see how great America is. You're off the project. You're fired, and you're going to jail. You're a nasty little idiot. I never liked you. In fact, you're not even a good scientist; you're a loser. A good scientist is the one who will make it $15 billion. I don't care what you have to do or what material you'll need to use, you'll make it for $15 billion."

The scientists loyal to him and his family worked at devising a blueprint for the largest aircraft to fly in the atmosphere or elsewhere in human history. It was called the Goliath.

The Goliath was sixty-four hundred feet in length, had a wingspan of seventy-five hundred feet, and weighed an impressive ten thousand two hundred forty tons.

Those who said it wouldn't recuperate its budget were

fools. After unveiling it to the world, Baron II was going to turn it into the most exclusive, most luxurious, most American hotel the world had ever seen.

There it was. Coming over the horizon, eclipsing the sun with its immensity. It was massive. The America of the skies. Nobody was laughing now. It shook the very foundations of the Earth. Baron II ordered it to fly as low to the ground as possible so those watching could tremble before it and admire its gargantuan nature.

We should have named it Gargantua. That goes so much harder than Goliath.

The world will tremble, Baron II thought. Armed guards stood at every exit, ready to intervene if any spectators felt an urge to be disrespectful and leave the venue early.

Baron II couldn't understand why they hadn't been building every airplane this big from the beginning. Nobody was afraid of normal size airplanes or fighter jets. He no longer cared that the tank and next-generation fighters had been duds. This was the greatest achievement in human history.

There was an unearthly sound of metals creaking and groaning. The left wing of the Goliath snapped off.

"Why did it do that?" Baron II asked.

Secretary Richter turned left and right. "Does anybody know whether the Goliath was supposed to lose debris?"

Multiple aides shrugged their shoulders. Others started making phone calls.

Not long after, the right wing snapped off. The airborne behemoth began to barrel roll, making impossibly long rotations. Then, the vessel cracked in half. The larger part of the cracked airship fell directly on top of the schools from Alabama through Kansas. The smaller part landed on the 101st Airborne Division. Altogether, the death toll was said to be upward of eight thousand.

All the scientists and engineers and physicists who worked on the plane were executed by means of the sword Machel had gifted the president.

2057

Reza got the phone call at three in the morning. The abrasive nature of the ringtone took him out of a pleasant sleep, and it was difficult to catch his bearings.

"I'll be right there," he assured the voice on the other end.

He never wanted to be an immigration lawyer, especially with immigration policy being in constant flux over the past five years. As soon as he starts answering one inquiry, the travel policy has already changed, and he has to delete the draft to start over.

He rode the metro to Hermann-Debroux Station. When he arrived at the office, the case manager was already waiting, impatient. There was freshly brewed synthetic coffee in the corner of the room. By 2050, the areas suitable for growing coffee had been reduced by sixty percent. Arabica had gone extinct. A one-kilo canister of coffee then cost around four hundred euros. Multiple synthetic derivatives emerged, with Nescafé being the most widespread. Having never tasted the real thing, Reza had no point of comparison, but by that same token, nothing to complain about. His case manager, fifteen years his senior, swore the difference in tastes and texture was radical. Typically taking it black, Reza put in an excessive amount of sugar to help with the waking-up process. Natural sugar had also been greatly reduced by climate change. All derivatives and artificial sweeteners were referred to as sugar by then.

It was hard for him to shake the feeling that he was a dead man walking based on the looks of his peers. The case manager himself did little to convince Reza otherwise.

"How interesting were you hoping your morning would get?" asked the case manager.

During his days as a paralegal, Reza vividly remembered when his superior asked him if he was ready for an interesting morning. For all their skills as litigators and solicitors, nearly every lawyer Reza had come across was an abysmal accountant. On that particularly interesting morning, Reza discovered that he was quite skilled at accounting. He was good enough to teach it to his superior, but not so good to miss a glaring mistake in the paperwork. That mistake caused his superior embarrassment in front of the judge. Reza had gotten off lucky; he only had a stapler thrown at his face. He got good at dodging them afterward.

"Interesting? Not very," said Reza.

"Drink your coffee and be effervescent, won't ya? You're going to need it. For the time being, all your casework is being handed off to Chloe."

"Did I do something wrong?" asked Reza.

"That's not it. We've got a problem that requires a...delicate touch. Initially, we thought it was an open and shut case, considering who the client is, but it's proving to be rather onerous. In Room 403, an American is waiting for you."

"That can't be," said Reza.

"I agree, but disregarding the impossibility of it all, there's an American sitting in Room 403 who believes it's entitled to the services of an attorney."

To Reza, hearing this information was akin to being told a unicorn had shown up in his back garden. The last he'd seen of Americans was footage tourists had taken on a safari in Botswana. The legality of it all was shaky. Every nation on Earth had unilaterally shut its doors to American refugees by 2045, and the European Union had closed its borders long before that in the 2030s. That didn't stop some countries from rounding up what Americans they could, those further along in the evolutionary process, and displaying them in farms, zoos, or safaris.

The Americans Reza had seen in the Botswana video were more than three hundred and twenty kilos and ran on all fours, not dissimilar from videos he'd seen of enormous hippopotamuses chasing after tourists. They were always nude, always massive, and always hungry. Sometimes, he speculated these videos had been doctored, aggrandizing just how far the American civilization had fallen.

Not all Americans had turned into those beasts. The United States was, theoretically, still a country, even if not a functioning one. Most nations had ceased all diplomatic relations and trade with the US. Multiple territories within the continental United States had been completely decimated by unrestricted drilling and resource mining. Deserts had been formed from once-forested areas. The parts of the country where sentient people still lived were rampant with crime and anarchy. The EU had banned all imports of US-based media, information, technology, entertainment, and so on. That didn't stop the president and ambitious Americans from trying to illegally broadcast their incomprehensible philosophy abroad.

"This American," said Reza. "Can it speak?"

"See for yourself."

Reza entered the room, expecting to see a horrific monster, but the person sitting opposite him wasn't all that dissimilar from him. A young man no older than twenty, with dark hair, a slim build, and eyes with comprehension.

Despite knowing the cut-and-dry legality of the affair, Reza wasn't disgusted by the sight of the American as he expected to be. Sitting before him, he couldn't help but think the young man could easily pass for a long-lost relative of his.

"Do you speak French? If not, I can speak English."

"How about Arabic?" asked the American in French.

"Unfortunately, that's not among my languages. How did you get to Belgium?"

"I was born in Belgium," he said.

Reza hoped his face wasn't betraying him, but he was feeling giddy conversing with an American. Before entering the room, he imagined being faced with some fat grotesquerie. All parents in Belgium used imagery of the scary American to frighten their children into behaving. The American Reza's father told bedtime tales of was a creature that had two heads, each always trying to get a bigger bite of slop from the other.

The conflicting heads would rather see the other die than share a meal together.

"That can't be. All the Americans were long ago rounded up. There was only ever one recorded outbreak of American herds roaming the streets of Antwerp before they were caught and deported. There were no more than four hundred here."

"I'm not American," he said.

There was no malice or defiance in his voice.

"According to European Union Law, an American is defined as anyone, up to and including those whose ancestors trace their heritage to United States citizenship back five generations. Debate as to which Americans, if any, aren't immune to the effects is ongoing."

"Do I not look immune to the effects?" he asked.

"The law is the law," said Reza. "According to the dossier, your great-grandparents moved to the US from Palestine, and your grandparents were born there. Then, when the American Refugee Crisis started, they were on the wave of immigrants who sought refuge in Europe."

"What if I can prove to you that, regardless of what citizenship is indicated on a document, I am not American?"

"How can you do that?" asked Reza.

"You haven't asked me my name," the young man said.

"You're right. My apologies. What is your name?"

"I'm Ali," he said.

"What is it you want from me, Ali?"

"All I ask is that you read this."

He handed Reza a stack of papers, all of which were in English. It appeared to be a compilation of several different sources: a thesis, publications, and the ramblings of a madman. The name at the top of all of them was Akseli Holopainen.

~~~

After returning to his native land, Akseli fell into obscurity. He never published anything of note and stopped updating his public blog in 2029. Had he been alive to see the current state of things, he likely would have felt validated at how accurate his predictions had been.

Reza spent his twenty-seventh birthday ingesting as much synthetic caffeine as he could get his hands on and poured over the words of Akseli Holopainen.

His piece stated:

It happened to Americans first, but that's not to say it can't happen again. The American brain, soul, mentality, whatever you choose to call it, was particularly susceptible, which is why the process began several generations earlier than my initial prognostications.

Nobody was ready to heed my warnings regarding the newly discovered neurotransmitter. Trying to make people take seriously a threat that they cannot see is like herding cats. If you can't see it, can't understand what you can't see, can't sell it, can't patent it, and can't market it, then it doesn't exist.

A neurotransmitter, invisible and with mysterious characteristics, whose origin is unknown, evolving into another invisible entity, meant nothing to anyone who had the power to study it, combat it, and prevent it from growing. By the time I
~~~

left the US, it was already too late. The neurotransmitter was evolving faster than I could study it.

Reza had some peers who got mild amusement from reading old blogs or watching videos from the early internet days. He never saw any utility in it. It was hard to relate to many of their mannerisms or cultural references. He found himself dozing off while reading Akseli's words but decided to power through it.

Did Americans create this neurotransmitter, or did the neurotransmitter make them what they are? Since its inception as a nation, the United States of America has held onto its obsolete form of strict puritanism and Manifest Destiny, the two biggest cornerstones of American thought. Add a good mix of White Anglo-Saxon Protestantism, rampant evangelicalism, and this is the glue that holds together and defines what it is to be American.

While other races, creeds, religions, and ethnicities may have cohabitated the continent, they did not prevail. They assimilated or remained outliers. Those that remained outliers, whether by virtue of being Catholic, agnostic, Sikh, or any other identity, prevailed in a way that prevented the neurotransmitter, or call it psychic forces, if that makes it easier to swallow, that bound Americans to one another from being affected.

Americans are particularly susceptible to pseudoscience, conspiracy theories, hocus pocus, astrology, and pretty much anything other than what has been scientifically proven. More Americans today believe the Earth is flat than people in the

Middle Ages did. More Americans believe angels exist than the idea of people having successfully landed on the moon.

One of my initial hesitations with presenting the new neurotransmitter to the public was the instinct telling me people would try to connect it to telepathy. Telepathy, as discussed by Reiser and Rice, was considered to be uncertain flashes, lacking in clarity, but flashes nonetheless of the coming groupmind, the world brain. But telepathy wasn't a power wielded by gifted talents. It was due to the American susceptibility to falsehoods and the belief in drivel that their empty minds were so easily infiltrated and conquered. This is why we won't see the effects of the transformation on a portion of the population who are American in name only.

Once the process started, it was too late to turn back. It happened gradually and beyond perception. If we see evidence of it happening, that means it's already too late.

Americans are losing their autonomy as individuals and forming a world brain, albeit an American one. What that will look like and how it will interact with the world at large is anyone's guess.

The process of forming the world brain won't be immediate. Americans will start to lose autonomy. As the neurotransmitter grows and changes, Americans may be reduced to animal-like entities that wander around, grazing. Or perhaps drone is a better comparison. They will lose the ability to speak and process information as individuals, because they are no longer individuals; they are neurons of a brain.

After several years of the beastlike grazing period, there will be the final transformation. It won't all happen simultaneously. Some will be affected earlier. Their bodies will become interconnected. It's possible that some Americans will bypass the beast stage, which could give them a false sense of security. Do not be fooled. Your autonomy will be short-lived.

What of the children of recent immigrants or refugees to the United States? Only time will prove me correct, but being American is not relegated to what the citizenship on one's passport says; rather, it concerns those who have been physically connected via the neurotransmitter. Therefore, Americans who adamantly believe in their own exceptionalism, manifest destiny, private healthcare, extortionist education costs, Christian nationalism, and think angels are real, those are the ones who will be affected.

When I am long dead and new generations have come and gone, I will be proven correct.

I can't be bothered.

Reza reviewed everything available on Akseli Holopainen. The neurotransmitter had been so neglected by experts and academia; it didn't even have a name.

Reza knew this was far too much to tackle on his own. Without any real hope of receiving a response, he sought the aid of Europe's top human rights lawyer, Roberto Piña. The fact that the famous Spaniard replied at all was nothing short of a miracle.

Did the possibly American entity known as *Ali* meet the statutory criteria of "American," as defined under the Continental Security and Purity Act (2055)?

Pursuant to Article 7 of the Act, the term *"American"* refers not solely to citizenship status as historically understood, but to *genetic, neurochemical, and memetic markers* derived from individuals originating in the former United States.

In the case of Ali—who did not display the genetic or physical characteristics associated with the so-called "beastly Americans" of the present—the Directorate's mandate was to determine whether such markers were present within the subject's biological or cognitive profile, thereby establishing whether the individual constituted a potential vector of *"American Contagion,"* defined as biochemical or ideological residues derived from exposure to the so-called Molecule USA.

After extensive research into ancestral ties to territories designated *Continental U.S.* between 1776 and 2039, and neurochemical analyses utilizing cross-scan comparisons of neurotransmitter composition against Control Group EU-A (baseline European brain chemistry) and Archive Group US-X (historical American neural samples)—along with dozens of other tests outside Reza's comprehension—the findings resulted in the following:

Ali's genealogical lineage displayed no traceable ancestral origin that was prevalent among the beastly Americans. His neurochemical composition presented no trace of the Molecule USA or any derivative neurosynthetics.

Reza and Roberto Piña were able to use these findings to reach a definitive legal conclusion regarding Ali's status. The subject did not meet the definitional or functional criteria of "American." His biological, neurochemical, and cognitive parameters were within acceptable deviation for certified human ancestry, with European Citizen of Neutral Ancestry (CENA) serving as the standard. Therefore, Ali posed no credible risk of American contagion.

He was not an American.

Did Reza dare make the findings public? What would it mean for the prosperous and unprecedented stability of the EU? The verdict had the potential to destabilize borders and economies. The hesitation stayed his hand for less than a minute.

~~~

After keeping Ali in a detention center for nearly eighteen months, enough lawyers, counselors, neuroscientists, and independent nongovernmental organizations reviewed the evidence and concluded he was not American.

Within minutes of the news breaking, Reza's office was swarming with people, seeking his legal guidance, hoping to prove they too were not American. Reza found himself the most in-demand lawyer in the EU.

New laws were drafted, and whether born in the United States or descended from US-born parents, formerly dubbed US citizens, after a quarantine period, were welcomed to the European Union.

Not all countries readily opened their borders. Japan still maintained a strict closed-door policy, but people who were once denied basic human rights were being treated as humans once more.

Picking up on Akseli's research, William Low from Glasgow University predicted the last sentient Americans would not only vanish within the next five years, but that it would be a rapid, large-scale event. The countdown began.
~~~

THE LAST AMERICANS

Whether out of jubilation or despair, for everyone, June 13 was a celebration. The streets outside of Baron II's Tower were a cacophony of gunshots, fireworks, explosions, motorcycles, and the chanting of death cults. From various skyscraper windows, priests were hanged and crucified. The people were laying the blame for their inevitable demise on America's false prophets.

Baron II could hear windows shattering on the floors of the tower below. More likely than not, his previously employed security detail was among those smashing the windows. All the building's employees had left to join the crowds or died trying to get to Baron II and his entourage.

The dynasty was meant to last over a thousand years. It had been started by his grandfather, yet it was to be his destiny to see it all come tumbling down.

"Try calling the Prime Minister once more," Baron II said, snorting from his mountain of cocaine on his glass table.

The week leading up to this day had been an orgy of booze, drugs, ceremonial killings, video game tournaments, and women. Baron II had clones of his favorite women with their genes altered to make them appear as different ethnicities of the same women. The fun took his mind off the impending doom momentarily, but the women kept overdosing on the fentanyl from the drugs before he could have his fun with them. He wondered why he wasn't OD'ing. He knew it was likely due to his superior genes, but then shouldn't that mean he was immune to what was to come?

The day before, his younger brother had jumped from the fortieth floor. Till the end, he tried to convince Baron II to come with him.

He drew his brother's face in the cocaine mound before inhaling.

"This is not how I die," he said. "Try calling the Prime Minister goddammit!"

Secretary of War Richter, whose hair had gone gray even if his mustache hadn't, was twitching like a little retard. "He won't answer our calls. I've called a million times. Nobody will take us in."

"Somebody will take us in. Don't they know who my grandfather is?"

"I've told them," he said.

Baron II put his face inside the mound of coke. He was starting to need to take more frequent hits with less satisfying returns.

"I feel the same as I ever did. This whole nonsense was a lie to scare us. What about you?"

"I feel the same, too, sir," said Health Secretary Kennedy.

"Yet here we are, true-blooded Americans. Why don't we go ahead and nuke Iran just to show them we aren't going away?" said Baron II.

"That would be sublime, sir, but Chief of Staff Montgomery took the launch codes to his grave."

"You're kidding? So, in my supposed final days alive, I have nothing to nuke Iran with?"

Baron II started what he thought was going to be a yawn but burst into tears.

"Sir?" asked Kennedey.

"Don't look at me!"

"Want some ketamine?"

"Yes, but don't look at me."

Baron II took some ketamine.

"How much time do we have left?" he turned his wrist so Kennedy could tell Baron II the time on his Rolex.

"I have a confession to make, sir, I never learned to read capital numbers."

"It just isn't fair. I didn't even get to bang the Puerto Rican clone. How is that fair?"

"It isn't."

"Are you afraid?" asked Baron II.

"Mr. President?" asked Kennedy.

"Do you believe in heaven or hell?"

"Of course, sir."

"Then maybe we should kill ourselves? The way my brother did. I don't want to transmorph, or whatever it is those motherfuckers said would happen. I've never even had sex with a redhead. Can you believe it? Even if we could call one down right now, I don't know if I'd be able to. I'm too depressed. My feelings are too complex."

"What can I do for you, Mr. President?" said Richter.

"Well, if we can't nuke anyone, we can still carpet bomb someone, can't we? Is there anyone still in the air taking orders?"

"It's all gone quiet, sir."

The president collapsed, his back to the corner of the room. Looking outside, he could see stacks of smoke everywhere. Screams, whether from jubilation or terror, carried through the air.

"I think I'm too scared for the drugs to do anything. I've never been scared a day in my life," said the president.

He pushed himself back onto his feet.

"No, it doesn't end like this. I am the president of the greatest country in the world, descended from the great American dynasty. I am chosen by God and by the people. I decide when it ends."

He picked up one of his various awards, some gold obelisk thing, and threw it at the window. Nothing happened.

"Goddamn bulletproof glass," he said.

"Richter, Kennedy, tomorrow we're going to look back on this day and laugh at how silly we were."

There was no response from the two men. The president turned around, and they were frozen, standing slack jawed.

"Well, say something,"

Their mouths were both open, as if to scream, but no sound came out.

"Say something, dummies."

Beads of sweat poured from their faces. Soon, so much

water was coming out from under their hairlines that the president initially took it for rain. The right half of Richter's face began to melt away, while the left half of Kennedy's began to do the same thing. Soon, skin and flesh were gone from the respective sides of their bodies.

Baron II wanted to smack them silly. "I will not tolerate this. Start acting like men, dammit!" *Why aren't they obeying their president?*

Tiny, nearly invisible tendrils began to grow out of their exposed brains, like small wires searching for something. Kennedy's tendrils connected to Richter's, and they began to wrap around one another.

"Stop that!"

The president tried to pull Kennedy away, but his body would not budge. Richter's mustache lay in a water flesh pile near the man's feet. He didn't want to get anywhere near the tendrils.

Then, the bodies were only inches from one another. The remaining flesh on their cheeks made contact.

"Don't you dare!" yelled the president.

The two men's faces began to merge, and soon it wasn't apparent where one face began and the other ended. Neither man blinked nor displayed any indication of pain or discomfort.

They shared one giant mouth, with one row of top teeth overlapping the other. New teeth grew over old teeth, while other teeth fell out. Their eyes struggled to find room in the newly formed head. They swam around like loose egg yolks in a bowl. Momentarily, there were three eyes in a line, with one floating above the top trying to squeeze its way through.

The president rushed to the window and began banging on it. *This type of shit happened in places like Rwanda or Canada, but not here. I don't condone this, and neither would my father or his father. I'm going to get a scientist, a loyal one, to put an end to this foolishness.*

"Damn you! Somebody get up here and stop this anti-American plot right now!"

All was quiet. *What happened to all the screams?*

Nobody would come to his aid. Down below, despite being on the fiftieth floor, he saw a giant mass of people floating slowly toward him.

He never paid much attention to arithmetic, but he guessed there were anywhere from a thousand to two thousand people, all connected or in the process of being joined by thin tendrils and merging into a meaty, fleshy ball. Liquids and flesh chunks fell away from the growing sphere of morphing human bodies. It was coming to him.

Parts of the growing mass of flesh broke away, hurling human blobs through the windows. Bodies morphed, melted, drooped, and clung together, as if uncertain where one ended and another began. Shapes rose and collapsed in slow motion, striving toward coherence but dissolving again into shimmering pools of flesh. As the blobs drifted closer to Baron II, they sometimes solidified into great, crablike forms—distorted parodies of life—only to lose their balance and slump apart. The corridors seemed to resist their passage, and so they melted once more, reforming in endless, desperate cycles, inching ever nearer to Baron II.

He ran up several flights of stairs, but each time he looked at the window, he saw the ball getting bigger and closer. What frightened him most was the silence. Nobody screamed. The last moments of all these individuals were deathly silent. The only sound was the unnatural gushing of tendrils ripping out of flesh to join other tendrils.

By the time he got to the top floor, his eyes were raw from crying. *I never cried a day in my life. What kind of sick shit is this? It's not my fault! None of this is my fault! I warned people for years. The lies and depravity of the opposition go so deep. There's no low they won't stoop to. I won't let them see me cry. It's not me who should be crying anyway, but them.*

"Not like this."

Baron II became aware of his brain. He had never before realized it was actually there, doing things. Now, he could feel it moving and activating inside. It was gross.

All around him, the glass shattered rhythmically, like a hellish orchestra closing in on him. The clamor was overpowered by the demonic sounds of bones bending, twisting, scraping, and shattering as tendrils, flesh, and skin tried to find leverage through all the broken glass and steel.

"It will not end like this!"

His face started to burn.

He let out a scream and tried to do something, but his arm wouldn't move.

Water began to spill down his face, just like he'd seen it do to Kennedy and Richter.

Neither of them had moved a muscle, leading him to believe there would be no pain, but he felt every excruciating moment of it. He could feel the skin leaving his face, the flesh underneath exposed to the stale air. He then felt as each cell broke apart and ran down his face. All the while, he could feel the tendrils not growing, but ripping out of his body, searching for their nearest neighbor.

Who is anyone to judge me? I am president because I am better. Anything I wanted to do was justified because I said it was. I am a superior person. The laws of God and man don't apply to me. This. Does. Not. Happen. To. Me. Should I beg for forgiveness? Say a prayer? Does a prayer count if I can't put my hands together?

Input from all the senses was folding in on itself, bleeding together until sight became scent, taste became touch, and nothing stayed in its proper place. He was seeing through someone else's eyes but smelling their sight, tasting the texture of what they touched. His ears could smell everything, and his eyes—his eyes wanted to vomit. The brains around him pulsed in time, millions of neurons drumming to a single rhythm, like a vast orchestra finding one impossible tempo. Dopamine and serotonin began to dance, spiraling into a circle that belonged to no one and everyone at once. He knew these thoughts couldn't be his—he had never known the names of those chemicals before today—yet they flowed freely through his mind, whispering what they were, what they were doing, and how peculiar it was that he could understand them. He felt them smoothing the edges between every mind, coaxing, seducing, promising glorious rewards if they would only surrender and merge.

He tried to remember his inauguration—the first moment he had stood before his people as their leader—but the memory slipped sideways. His speech returned in Spanish, then fractured into a dozen other tongues, until his mind was a storm of languages, every one of them familiar and foreign, none of them his own. He could no longer recall the name of the language he once spoke.

The voices rose around him, clamoring, luminous, each demanding his attention. He could smell their words, and they tasted unbearably loud.

While that was going on, he started to see...everything. He felt the thoughts and feelings of every person, first those of his aides, then those of the flesh ball outside, and then those of people connected by tendrils all across the country. Every fear, every anxiety, everything. Amplified. So loud. Make it stop! They hated his name. No matter how much he hated someone, it couldn't compare to their loathing of him. Each disappearing cell captured the feeling of hatred and copy and pasted it through the growing mass of flesh. In addition to that, he felt other fears and anxieties being pasted into his consciousness. They hated him so much. They hated his father, and his father, and all the fathers in his lineage going back.

That couldn't be. All his life, he was told he was loved. *Someone couldn't be president unless they were loved; it was a simple fact (unless they were from the opposing side).* There was no one there, nobody at all, to tell him they loved him. To tell him it was going to be okay. He tried to yell at them, but no one would listen. All that remained was an overwhelming abhorrence of all things that were his family.

When the faces of women and the names of family vanished, he could remember fear. Each second became a millennium. As an autonomous individual, his final thoughts were of intense fear, anxiety, and self-loathing. Even once his body was fully absorbed and his ego no longer existed, that sense of fear and hatred of all things that were his family remained lost somewhere within the ever-growing ball. It all occurred in less than a millisecond, but to him it was an eternity.

In total, 370 million Americans ceased to be. When all was said and done, it took two and a half years for the brain to be complete. Once all the bodies were gathered, it made several attempts at reconfiguring itself until it resembled what was unmistakably a giant brain.

All attempts at communication ended in failure. It merely remained stationary at its home in Yellowstone National Park. The brain was roughly the size of a football field.

Initially, some animals, such as wolves and bears, came up to sniff it, but eventually grew bored and left it alone.

The surviving Americans found themselves not knowing what would come next. Did their country even exist anymore? Were they truly immune?

The brain neither attacked nor defended itself when scientists attached electrodes to it, trying to gauge any sort of response or reaction.

Some people feared that, although it only affected Americans, it didn't rule out the possibility of it happening to someone else one day. Increasingly, thoughts like this ingrained themselves all around the world. Whether as an act of mercy or a pre-emptive first strike, some believed the brain should be destroyed. Other factions believed it best to leave the brain alone, while others yet thought it should be launched into space or sunk deep into the Marianna Trench.

There was a contingent of surviving, autonomous Americans who pushed for communicating with the brain, hoping to find signs of their family or loved ones inside the organism. Some nations believed resisting evolution was the wrong move, and efforts should be made to propel the losing of individual autonomy and forming a giant national brain. Most of the world took the opposite approach, opting instead to study where Americans had gone wrong and to do everything in their power to avoid a similar fate.

There was another faction, initially small in number, whose vision eventually spread across continents. They saw in the brain proof of Nikolai Fyodorov's "common task." To them, the brain represented the beginning of the world envisioned by the nineteenth-century Russian ascetic. Fyodorov, who regarded the principles of the French Revolution as shallow, held a far grander ideal for humanity. The "common task" required society to strive in all its endeavors—technologically and spiritually, politically and scientifically—to serve this ultimate goal of obtaining eternal life for all of mankind. A reunion of every soul that had ever lived and died with those yet to live and perish themselves.

Followers of this belief saw a means of cheating death. Even if they did not yet fully understand how, they believed the answers to resurrection—and the possibility of reuniting with their loved ones—lay within the American brain. Rather than being something to fear, their belief held that all research should be immediately devoted to creating brains throughout the world until all populations, everywhere, formed one vast world brain.

Expeditions of scientists, researchers, and artists who came to study the brain often reported feeling an intense sickness from being near it for extended periods of time. They often left with intense feelings of brain fog and couldn't remember simple concepts like basic math or left from right. After being quarantined, the effects eventually wore off.

This phenomenon led many to believe that the brain was contagious, causing large-scale support for its destruction. Furthermore, the era of American hegemony had come to a swift end. Power dynamics in geopolitics shifted, as did alliances and borders. What the new world would look like frightened people just as much as it enticed them. By the year 2065, the debate on what to do with the brain was still ongoing.

ACKNOWLEDGMENTS

I would like to express my sincere and eternal gratitude to the following people: Keary Iarussi, Austin Wilson, Fergus Gregg, Marshall David, Chris Cortez, Chris Hernandez, Eshawn Rawlley, Robin Fuller, Laila Ali, Mary Haley Ousley, Veronica Anez, Lee Quinn, Merryn Post, Anja Peerdeman, Keeley McCormack, Chase Philpot, Kerry Bates-Redler, Jelena Medic, Alfred Obare; editors Karen Brown and Nicholas Carter; my mother and various aunts and uncles; and, finally, all the people who choose to remain anonymous but helped nonetheless. Thank you.